I0690175

MY, WHAT TICKLISH FEET YOU HAVE

First Edition

Published by The Nazca Plains Corporation
Las Vegas, Nevada
2012

ISBN: 978-1-61098-292-4
E-book: 978-1-61098-293-1

Published by

The Nazca Plains Corporation ®
4640 Paradise Rd, Suite 141
Las Vegas NV 89109-8000

PUBLISHER'S NOTE
My, What Ticklish Feet You Have is a work of fiction created wholly
by James T. Medak's imagination. All characters are fictional and
any resemblance to any persons living or deceased is purely by
accident. No portion of this book reflects any real person or events.

Feet Photo, Valeriy Lebedev
Feathers Photo, Sikth
Art Director, Blake Stephens

MY, WHAT TICKLISH FEET YOU HAVE

First Edition

James T. Medak

DEDICATION

TO BASTIAAN, THE LOVE OF MY LIFE.

CONTENT

INTRODUCTION

It's certainly an odd thing to say, but feet are pretty darn sexy.

While someone without a foot fetish may not necessarily understand the appeal, foot fetishism is actually one of the most common fetishes in the world. In fact, more than one third of all body fetishes (both male and female) involve feet in some way. While the average person may not find removing their socks after a long day of work very sexy, what they're missing is the intimacy of it all. People (aside from hippies) don't go barefoot very often, so to be around someone who is unshod is to be around someone who is vulnerable. Being barefoot around someone creates a strange sense of intimacy, of trust – and that, in and of itself, is kind of sexy.

Society almost demands that we be teased with this very fact, as strapped sandals have given way to gloriously cheap flip-flops, and what was once considered a "lazy look" is now very much considered the norm. Seeing a guy in flip-flops and jeans is one of the most killer looks I've ever seen, and while it may have been a rarity when I was younger, it's damn near commonplace now, and seeing a whole range of straight boys adopt this fashion template stirs up nothing but wonderful, devious thoughts inside of me. The nice thing about having a foot fetish is that it can be combined with other fetishes pretty easily (it's the Transformers of fetishes), ranging from gunge to balloons to, of course, tickling. I very proudly have a male foot and tickle fetish, and figured that after writing a book called *How to Be a Tickle Slave*, it was time to write stories that had a bit more sole. There are, of course, copious amounts of tickling still to be had here in *My, What Ticklish Feet You Have*, but figured that with a compendium like this, we should just integrate the very best of both worlds…

So do enjoy fair reader (and it should go without saying that you yourself should be shoeless while glancing at these pages). To everyone who supported me through the first book (and all those on the forums), thank you. Young, ticklish Kyle, especially, gets help for making this book what it is (see: readable). Michael K. and William get personal shoutouts from me for creating some gloriously lust worthy images, and cheerleaders like Ian Marshall and Joey (yes, you) are worthy of high, ticklish hurrahs. To everyone in my life who directly inspired these characters – most rather unknowingly – my hats off to you (please continue wearing exactly what you wear on a daily basis). To everyone who wrote to me, contacted me, or just all-around helped me out as a writer with kind words and encouragement following the first book, let me be frank and honest: thank you. You have no idea how much those words have meant to me. Seriously, you're awesome.

Now, if you don't mind, I have some tickling to get to…

James T. Medak
August 2011

CHAPTER ONE

THE BELT

I honestly have never been that much into chastity. I can understand the appeal of it, but to have to go through prolonged periods of time without orgasm, much less a hard-on – that's rough. However, I find it very interesting the way that pleasure can be delayed like that, and how after a good long period of time, the horny mind can become delirious, exasperated, and ready for anything. When thinking about that idea, I just wondered how long someone could take it before they went completely bonkers...

"Fuck man, I'm gonna cum!" moaned out Michael, almost desperately, bathed in nothing but the glow of his computer monitor. He stood there, jerking off furiously to the image that stood before him: a webcam screen that was filled with the soles of Benjamin, his long-time net friend and owner of the most glorious pair of feet he had ever seen, lightly toned and massive in their size 13 stature. All Ben had done was simply prop his big bare feet in front of the webcam on his desk, and slowly began rubbing his feet together. Michael – thin frame, lightly shaggy brown hair, and owner of an unbelievably intense male foot fetish – was in sheer ecstasy, about to cum merely from the sight of Ben's perfect feet. Ben somewhat unconsciously twitched his toes, and that was enough to set Michael off: that intense electric feeling at the very tip of his cock manifested itself in a furious stream of cum; so intense that Michael – not expecting for that toe twitch to do what it did – jizzed all over his desk, some even getting on his keyboard. As embarrassed as he was going to feel in a few moments, his cock – hell, his whole body! – radiated a tingle of pleasure that he had not felt in some time.

Of course, Michael's webcam was on, too, and Ben saw everything. Ben took his feet down from his computer desk and watched from his own computer window as Michael took a few moments to gather his thoughts – his cock gradually deflating as Michael appeared, well, dumbstruck. Michael spoke into his mic: "I'll be right back. Let me clean up."

"No problem," said Ben, slyly. He watched as Michael grabbed some paper towels from his apartment bathroom, and soon cleaned everything up. Ben spoke to Michael as he did so:

"Quite the load this time, man."

"That toe twitch near the end… that's what did me in. I don't really know it just… gah, it was so fucking sexy."

"Man, I *love* how deep your foot fetish is. It's pretty intense."

"That *cumshot* was pretty intense, dude." Michael threw the paper towel away and sat down in front of his desk, his face now in perfect frame for the webcam. It was night out, so the only thing that was illuminating him was a lamp off to the side.

Michael sat there, looking at the large, heavy cardboard box that was next to his chair on the ground. He asked Ben upfront: "Can I open it?"

"In a moment," said the dusty-haired hunk on the other end. "But first, let me ask you: you love my feet, right?"

"Yes."

"And... just using your best guess... how many times have you cum to my feet? Including our little web chat tonight?"

"Geez... dozens, easy. Maybe even close to a hundred, even."

"That's good, Michael. I hope you know that I *love* how horny my feet make you."

Michael smiled a bit, genuinely pleased with that statement. "Thanks, Ben."

"Now, here's the question: what is *my* fetish?"

"You have a male tickle fetish sir."

"Now, how many times have I tickled you?"

"Well, none, really. I know you want to tickle me, but I... I hate being tickled."

"And what have I asked of you before?"

"To... to fly out for a tickle session?"

"Well," clarified Ben, "a tickle *and* foot session. You'd get to worship my dogs in person, you lucky devil you."

Michael smiled again. "Well, yes, but you know me – I work at a friggin' KFC. You're at an architecture firm now. You, naturally have a bit more cash than me."

"And I've offered to fly you out."

"I know, but, well, it's kind of hard to plan these things."

"But!" started Ben. "I think I have a way to fix it."

"Oh you do?" asked Michael, genuinely curious.

"And it's in that box."

"Can... can I open it now?"

Ben smirked. "Yes, yes you can, Michael – but put it in your lap. I want to see your reaction as you open it.

Michael smiled, and then lifted the too-heavy cardboard cube onto his lap. He got out his scissors and cut open the taped flaps at the top. He flipped the flaps down, tossed a ton of packing peanuts onto the floor, and then stared at it… confused.

"What is it?" asked the 23-year-old lad.

Ben – only one year older than him – smirked back. "Take it out."

Michael did – and it was some sort of, well, belt thing. It was metal, and appeared to be something you place around the hips. There were metal straps that seemed to hug the inner thighs of each leg, but nothing on the back, which made it still OK to use the restroom should one want to. Yet, what was on the front is what scared Michael: a hard plastic sort of pocket that seemed perfectly shaped to house… his junk. This whole thing looked very professionally tailored (soft fabric on the insides so there's no chaffing), but it also seemed like it could lock very easily as well. There was a small panel that had a spinning four-digit lock combination (each little wheel with the numbers 0-9 on them), but all were set at 0 for the time being.

Michael looked blankly into the webcam and asked quite simply: "What is it?"

Ben smiled back: "It's a chastity belt."

"Why… why would you get me a chastity belt?"

Ben smiled, and coyly lied to his online friend: "Well, I thought it could make things more exciting."

"What do you mean?"

"My feet are the hottest you've seen, right?"

"No question."

"Well, think of it as a loyalty thing. This orgasm tonight was the best yet, right?"

Michael blushed a little. "Well… yeah."

"Then put it on, and in three days, I'll give you the code. We'll see how horny you get after two days of not being able to jerk it."

Michael thought for a moment… and liked the idea. The idea of "saving himself" for his secret foot master, his dick being owned only by him, begging for release after two days of not being able to do it. Michael didn't have anything else really going for him, thought, *why not?*

"Sure." He said. Looking at the screen, he saw Ben light up with a gigantic smile.

Ben responded: "I want to see you put it on over the cam and lock it."

"Alright!" said Michael, a bit excited by the possibility.

With that, Michael dropped his pants and shorts, but still kept on his solid-red hoodie. Ben had previously remarked how much he liked Michael in that hoodie, which is why Michael made sure to wear it every time they cam'd together. With his body half-naked, he placed the chastity belt on the ground and stuck his legs in the holes between the outer-rim and those inner-thigh hugger deals (which, at least to him, made sense as to where he should put his legs). He slid the thing up like a metallic pair of shorts, and it reached to his hips.

"Wow… this thing is snug, Ben. Like… it fits almost perfectly."

"Well I once asked for your measurements. I'm not sure if you remember, but I certainly did. This thing has been custom made to fit you."

"Well… well thanks, man."

"Don't worry about it. Now, here's the important part: when putting your junk in the front, make sure it fits comfortably."

Michael heeded this advice as he adjusted and maneuvered his balls in place. Finally, it felt pretty cozy.

"Alright. I think I'm good."

"Excellent," said Ben. "Now, turn it so that your right side is facing the cam, and let me see you lock it in place."

Michael did so. There were two metallic little "pieces" on the right side that were usually held together by a bit of stretchy fabric, allowing the wearer to fit in without having it already locked in place. Michael brought the two interlocking ends together, and they clicked into place. Boom. He was now wearing a chastity belt.

"I think it's ready to roll, Ben!"

"Alright – now try to take it off."

Michael arched his eyebrow. "Um… OK."

Michael tried pulling it down… but it was no go. The thing was locked above his hipbones, so he was now pretty secure. He tried a few different angles, but… nothing.

"Nope, locked in pretty securely, Ben."

"Alright," said his smiling friend. "I'll catch you later then."

And then their chat was disconnected.

Michael sat there – in nothing but his hoodie and chastity belt – and was a bit shocked by the suddenness of Ben's disappearance. After a few moments, he realized that his friend meant nothing personal by his sudden disappearance and that in a few days' time, they'd cam again, and Michael would be as horny as ever, and the resulting orgasm would be nothing short of spectacular. Having already drained himself quite exhaustively, Michael went to bed feeling pretty pleased that night. Took a bit for him to get used to the belt, but after about an hour, all was good.

Although showering was a bit weird, Michael was slowly getting used to the belt. Within the first hour of his KFC shift, behind the register while the smell of refried chicken permeated behind him, Michael felt a bit… naughty. He kind of smiled a bit, knowing that he was keeping a secret that no one else knew. The idea kind of got him a little horny for the first time since his cam session last night but… it wasn't going. His hardon wasn't materializing. In fact, it kind of hurt that his cock was being pressed up against the hard plastic shell that contained his junk. Michael stepped away from the register for a second – prompting one bucket-ordering soccer mom to ask if he was OK – but after a bit, he got his grip on things, and was able to continue his job as per usual. He didn't realize that a sharp pain like that was all it would take for his erection to go away. He had one more "erotic wave" hit him like that near the end of his shift, but for the most part, his chastity belt was still a pretty fun idea.

That night, after getting back to his small apartment and working on his long-gestating children's book (which he's rewritten about 10 times now), he started feeling a bit needy. He opened up his folder containing all of the hot foot worship picks he had gotten off the web, and began browsing through them, his finger unconsciously circling his plastic cock cage. After a bit, he got a bit horny, but then came the pressing plastic pain, and he didn't. Suddenly, Michael realized that he was experiencing true sexual frustration. Not just that he wasn't getting blown or anything, but that when he wanted to jerk himself off – which he did twice daily, usually – he wasn't able to. He was getting a little mad that he wasn't able to, but, hey, Ben said he'd be online in a day or two anyways. No big deal. Having not cum, it was a bit harder for Michael to sleep that night, but he did so anyways.

On his third day, Michael was getting a little bit flustered. Although day two saw him kind of at the limits of what he was capable of experiencing, this was now getting kind of crazy. He hadn't cum in at least three days, and, for him, that was some new sort of record. Around his co-workers he got kind of testy, but he was still in control. That night, upon getting home, he loaded up his webcam first thing and just waited. Ben was going to come on any second now. He looked at some pictures in his folder just to get himself ready and – to taper off his frustration – he began walking around the apartment just to burn off some energy. An hour passed with nothing. Michael popped in a DVD into his computer (boy did he love *The Office*), and watched one episode in a reduced screen, one eye always lingering on his webcam just to see if Ben was online and connecting. One episode turned into two, then two into three. After Michael had watched an entire disc, he broke out his cell phone and sent a text to Ben, asking where he was. Ten minutes passed, and no response. Michael popped in another disc of that same season of *The Office*, and barely even watched the entire thing, as he kept glancing at his phone every twenty seconds, followed by his webcam at every other interval. Nothing. After the third episode on the second disc, suddenly his phone vibrated! IT WAS BEN! he thought. He flipped open the phone, and it was... a message from Tim, his best friend. He was asking if Michael was up for another pub crawl tomorrow night (that night being Friday). Michael and Tim *always* hit a new bar on Friday, but... what if he missed a session from Ben? Michael texted back saying that he'll "play it by ear"... but that's all he could promise now. A whole third disc of that same *Office* season was watched, but by the end, Michael knew his fate: Ben wasn't going to be on tonight – and he wasn't going to get to cum.

Michael took an extra-long shower that night, his body tingling with a certain kind of frustration that he hadn't known. Cumming was just about all he could think about right now, regardless of what the stimulus was. Hell, he'd have sex with a woman, even! As long as he got that thing off. His head swimming with horny ideas, Michael only got two hours of sleep that night.

The next night, after another frustrating day at work and having sent off at least THREE texts to Ben (all unanswered), Michael finally consented to a pub crawl with Tim. It was the start of April, after all – what could a little drink hurt? Maybe he'd even get so drunk that he'd forget about his horny predicament... at least for one night.

Michael eventually found his way to a downtown place called McGuillicuddy's, a pseudo-Irish place that seemed to have a bunch of barflies wearing trucker caps. He awaited by a small table next to the jukebox, and after a minute, his buddy Tim walked in: white ball cap, white T-shirt (which, suitably showed off his muscled arms), ratty blue jeans and... flip-flops. Tim had never, ever, ever worn flip-flops. Michael almost gasped as Tim walked over to hug him in that frat-brotherly way.

"What's going on, Mikey?"

"Oh," started Michael, meekly, "Nothing. Just a long, long day at work."

"Hell, I hear ya man," said Tim, sitting down. "Let's get some beers and forget about it, OK?"

Michael nodded, but couldn't help and glance under the table. Tim's feet were... fantastic. They were gloriously pale, thin and veiny, which contrasted nicely to Michael's too-rich memory of Ben's, which were rich and meaty. That said, Tim's feet still had an incredible charm to them. The more Michael delved into his fetish, the more he found certain unique pleasures to be found in the shape of each and every foot he came across. The fact that he had never seen Tim's before only intrigued him further, and now that he was staring at them, he felt awash in a certain kind of lust for them, something which was making his wearing of his chastity belt all the more inconvenient.

Then, Tim's hand was under the table, and it formed a finger pointing up. Oh shit – Michael had just been found out.

He arched his head back topside, and Tim was staring at him with one of his eyebrows prominently arched. "Um… what were you doing, Michael?"

"I… I couldn't help but notice you were wearing flip-flops."

"Well, yeah."

"You… never worn them before."

"I know, man. I went to the store with Donna just a few days ago, and figured 'why the hell not?' ya know? Worth trying something new. They're pretty fun to wear, actually."

"Yeah, they look good on you."

"… 'They look good on me'?"

"Well… I kinda… just…"

"What kind of statement is that?"

Michael got flustered and was definitely feeling cornered. This was his friend for several years, but… maybe it was time to be honest with him about it.

"Well, I'm sorry dude, but… I got a bit of a… foot fetish."

Tim's eyebrow arched again. "A foot fetish?"

"Yeah."

"For like, all feet or just… guys feet?"

"Guys feet."

Suddenly a waitress came over and handed off a round of beers. Tim thanked her and Michael barely had the strength to lift his arm to grab his, his whole body racked with guilt over this confession. Tim took a swig of his beer, and leaned in a bit, making a gesture for Michael to lean in as well. Tim spoke softly: "So… what would you want to do them?"

Now Michael was the one with the quixotic look on his face. "Pardon?"

"If we were alone right now and you could, I dunno, 'indulge' – what would you want to do to my feet?"

Michael scanned Tim's face for malice – and there was none. He genuinely wanted to know. For the first time in days, Michael smiled, and began spilling his guts.

Over the next two hours, the guys consumed about five beers apiece, and Michael told Tim all about his fetish: how it started, whose feet in particular he wanted to worship, and how Michael theorized this all stemmed from a psychological need to be subservient in sexual play, and licking the bared soles of a guy's feet was the ultimate subservient gesture. Tim ate it all up, smiling the whole time and even tossing in some questions of his own. Michael wasn't as much horny as he was happy, and the booze was *definitely* opening up his treasure chest of secrets. The evening bore on, and when the guys – very tipsy – turned to look at the football game on the big screen behind the bar, Tim slid his right foot out of his sandal and placed it right in Michael's lap. He turned a bit and simply said "rub it" off the side of his mouth. The guys drank and carried on a conversation just as normal, Michael eagerly rubbing his friend's foot the whole time. It felt… good.

As the bar began closing up around 1:30AM, Tim admitted that he was kind of feeling a bit kinky from all this open talk, and wondered if they wanted to go back to Michael's place to do something about it. The very mention of it – a long-standing fantasy of Michael's – was enough to drive him overboard. His erection was immediate – and halted just as immediately by his plastic encasement. He admitted to Tim that the offer was "tempting", but it best to wait for another time. Tim seemed a bit disappointed with the news, but secretly knew it was for the best. As Tim went off to hail a cab, Michael grew frustrated by the biggest missed opportunity of his life, and stomped his way home.

Jumping right into his e-mail, he fired off an angry missive towards Ben, saying how this whole chastity belt thing was not what he signed up for and that the code for unlocking it be given to him now, further explaining of the opp he just missed out on with Tim (the whole document riddled with typos and spelling errors, a mixture of both Michael's rage and drunken state of being). Michael hit Send and felt pretty good… until about five seconds later when he got a message back. It was from Mail-return-sender. Ben's e-mail address no longer existed. Michael checked his screen name on AIM, his webcam service, and everywhere: Ben wasn't online or was simply gone. Michael went to bed in a state of rage and frustration.

Being Saturday, Michael woke up about noon, and staggered around wearing just the belt. He put on some pajama pants and T-shirt so he could go check his mail, and opened the door to his apartment. There was another cube cardboard box simply sitting there. Michael inspected it: it was from Ben.

Frantically, Michael closed the door behind him and brought the cube into his living room area, setting it down on the couch before promptly ripping it open. It felt lighter than the previous package, and then, finally, Michael saw the contents: inside a tightly sealed Ziploc bag, there were two pairs of Ben's worn socks. As exciting as the revelation made him, he searched for a note, for a sign, for anything. Nothing. Just a Zip-locked bag filled with the used socks of his favorite foot god. Lacking anything else to do, Michael opened up the bag, and immediately the fumes hit him. They worked right into his nervous system, and right into his pleasure center. Michael was officially turned on. Even as his cock pressed furiously against the plastic of his belt, Michael didn't care for a little while: he was enjoying the moment.

For about an hour, Michael rolled on his bed smelling every inch of Ben's socks, his hand circling his plastic cock cage as he indulged what was essentially a horny feast for the senses. Michael simply couldn't control himself. He had never gone this long without cumming, and was awash in just about any hope he had of getting to PleasureTown. After that hour, though, Michael realized he wasn't going to get off, and got frustrated all over again. He revisited the richly textured socks frequently over the weekend, but to no use. As erotically charged as those playthings were, nothing would come of them.

Another week passed.

Michael finally was getting used to peeing through the little hole in the plastic cock cage, but that was about all he was getting used to. With each passing hour of him not getting off, the longer the days seemed to drag on. Someone at work simply mentioning "feet" – even if it's just in a sentence like "we got a line of customers 10 feet deep" – was enough to retrigger his fantasies all over again. Michael even contemplated going to a blacksmith to get the infernal device off, but his lack of funds – and sheer embarrassment over what that would look like – was enough to keep him away from that idea. With each passing day, his anger and frustration turned into defeat and frustration. That next Friday, he wound up crying himself to sleep he was so desperate. He frequently looked up the photos that Ben had sent him, and all they did was stir those romantically horny feelings he had for those massive feet all over again. It was an endless cycle.

On Saturday morning, Michael opened up his door and found another package at it: this time smaller. Opening it up, it was Ben's old, worn, leather flip-flops. Ben said that he had worn them for years – and it showed. Bit of fringing on the side, a definite worn shape to them, and, dear god, the most perfectly sweat blackened imprints of Ben's feet that Michael had ever seen. Looking at them, he didn't realize just how big Ben's feet were in real life. He brought the sandals to his nose, and inhaled. God, these were even MORE potent than the socks, having locked away almost five whole years of foot sweat inside of them. Horny and desperate, Michael licked the area where Ben's soles were, and the taste drove him mad. Despite his inability to get an erection, Michael couldn't help himself and licked both pairs of flips for whole hour-long lengths of time, relishing the taste like he was starved for a month and finally offered a juicy steak. The socks lost their potency, but these bad boys didn't. For yet another horny week, this was all Michael had to hold onto, and he did so with an almost psychotic desire. The belt had broken him, and he was now simply a slave to his own desires.

After what was the longest week of his life, Michael was up at 6AM the following Saturday, bright and early, sitting right next to the door of his apartment, waiting for a package to be dropped off while each second slowly ticked away. Ben's socks and flips were clearly out of sight, lest they trigger another frenzied licking session. At 10:07AM exactly, a package was dropped off. Waiting for the mailman to walk away a bit, Michael finally opened the door and saw that this package... was the smallest yet. It was a little bigger than an envelope, but it was still a package. With a fury rarely seen in a human being before, Michael opened up the package, and saw… a plane ticket. A single plane ticket. To Chicago O'Hare. Ben lived in Chicago. Ben had paid for Michael to come out there and visit him… and possibly unlock that belt once and for all.

Michael careened with joy. This was the best news possible! Finally, after three weeks of frustration, he'd finally get to worship the feet of his master! Wait a second… Michael was calling Ben his master in his mind. He really *was* broken. No matter. This was big news. Then, Michael actually took a second to read the ticket: the flight took off tomorrow. And there was no return ticket either. Michael flipped out his phone and sent a message to Ben noting that he couldn't get the time off of work for a visit like that (keep in mind, this was a nice change of tone to the last 100 unanswered text messages that Michael had sent out that week, the last two being 'dear fuck you are my god i want to lick your solezz' and 'i will do anything for the chance to worship you, sir'). The message, naturally, went unanswered. He then got dressed and headed down to his KFC to talk to his manager about it.

After not getting a day off to attend a "family emergency", Michael quit right then and there. Perhaps it was a good thing there was no return ticket: Michael would never want to come back here anyways.

The very next day, Michael found himself in mid-flight, staring out at the white fluffy clouds before him and wondering what the hell he was doing. He thought about how he met Ben via an online web chat 'lo those many years ago, when they both were about 17. They both were kind of coming into their fetishes with each other, and though Michael hated being tickled and Ben wasn't as much a fan of worshipping feet (he did, however, like getting *his* feet worshipped), the boys found mutual ground and frequently discussed their victories and failures openly with each other, initially in regards to their fetishes, but increasingly about their lives as well. Ben was a bit unsure when Michael asked if he could see his bare feet for the first time, but upon seeing his reaction, Ben grew to enjoy the power that his toes held over Michael. Then again, Ben was a no-nonsense guy and it made sense that he would enjoy little hints of power. He slept with women, sure, but to tie a guy down and break him, to destroy his mind through the very act of tickling his ribcage… that was a kind of power that was special. Being who he is, Ben convinced lots of guys (straight ones even) to succumb to his tickling whims, but he always seemed to be on the prowl for the unwilling, the ones who you really had to coarse to get to do something like that. Ben liked challenges, and maybe Michael – the very first person he spoke to about his fetish – was the ultimate challenge, these plans years in the making. A college graduate but recently jobless, Michael wasn't sure what he was doing. This was all strange, but all new. He was as scared as he was excited to feel the plane wheels touch down in Chicago, not knowing what would happen next.

After getting his small bit of luggage from a baggage carousel, Michael stood in the airport (still wearing that red hoodie Ben loved so much); facing the glass doors leading out to the streets… and then realized that Ben didn't specify anything about was to happen now. Was Ben supposed to meet him here? Was he going to sneak up behind him and poke his sides in the airport? What if Ben was wearing flips? All those thoughts caused stirrings in his belt, but it's that very belt which put a stop to those stirrings. Then, suddenly, Michael felt his phone vibrate. He flipped it open – it was a text message from Ben. It said that there was a cab outside from Blue Taxi, its door open, and it had already been paid with directions right to Ben's loft apartment. Excited, Michael hurriedly called Ben, expecting him to be on the other end of the phone… but simply got voicemail. Ben was teasing him. Michael stood on the balls of his feet and looked out: there was, in fact, a cab, door open, waiting for him. Within two minutes time, Michael was gone.

He was dropped off in a nice high-rise just out of downtown Chicago. He went into the lobby, dragging his bags, and received another text message: "13th floor, room 1307". Excited and scared, Michael got in an elevator and made his way up. He got out at the 13th floor and ran through the carpeted hallways, looking for 1307. As he ran along, Michael noticed art hung up in certain areas and nice lighting everywhere – this was a really flashy place. Finally, Michael got to a door with "1307" across the front. He set his bags down, nervous, and knocked on the door. It opened almost instantaneously.

It was Ben. Ben was smiling.

"How goes it, Michael?"

Michael stood there and thought about all the things he could say to Ben right now, about how he's gone an entire month without jerking off, about how he missed out on the greatest worship opportunity ever with his good friend Tim because of the damn belt, and how the socks and sandals that were sent (which, Michael would be loath to admit, were in his luggage right now) did nothing but drive him up the wall. But when he saw Ben standing there – short brown hair, firm (but not flashy) build, and (dammit) some blue Chuck Taylors on his feet, coupled with how Michael has been able to trust Ben with virtually all of his secrets and was personally responsible for close to 100 orgasms for him personally – Michael just felt all that aggression melt away. This guy was his genuine friend… and he sure as fuck better get him off soon.

"It goes well, Ben." The two guys hugged. Ben motioned him in, and Michael looked around: there was hard wood paneling on the floors, an *island* fireplace, and some real nice couches. Ben had always mentioned that he made a decent hunk of cash from his fresh-out-of-college architecture job, but Michael never realized it was this much. No wonder he could also afford one-off plane tickets, crazy mailing fees, and even a custom-made chastity belt. Michael set his stuff down near the entrance.

"Really nice place you got here, Ben."

"Thank you Michael."

There was a bit of a pause between the boys, somewhat awkward. Michael started…

"So…"

"The belt." Ben cut him off. "I've received all your text messages. From what I guess, it's been driving you a little crazy."

Michael immediately dropped to his knees and began pleading "Holy shit you have no idea how insane this has been! I'm horny as I've ever been in my life and will do anything to get off oh please oh please oh please!"

Ben smiled a too-knowing smile at Michael.

"So you'll do anything for me to get that belt off of you?"

"Yes."

"And, I assume… you would like to worship my feet, is that right?"

"It's the only thing that's gotten me through this past month. I know their smell and their taste so well now – all I want is just to suck on your toes for hours, days on end."

"Alright. That sounds fair." Michael grinned the biggest grin he had ever donned. "But…"

"But?"

"You have to do me a favor first. You're going to get me off in exchange for the dozens of times I've gotten you, OK?"

Michael shocked yet resigned to his fate, simply said "OK. What do you want me to do, sir?"

Ben grinned again: "My bedroom is in the hallway on the right. I'll be in in two minutes, by which point I want you down to your boxers – and that hoodie of yours. Sound good?"

"Yes sir." said Michael, who marched on off.

Michael stood there and admired Ben's big, comfy bed. You really have to hop on up to get on it, but boy did that mattress look wonderful. As Michael examined, there appeared to be leather cuffs attached to each corner of the bed, but that's just when Ben walked in.

"Admiring those?"

"Well," Michael stammered, "I…"

"Don't worry. You'll get to know them real soon in a moment anyways. Now lie down in a spread eagle position face-up."

Wordless, Michael did so. Soon, Ben pulled out adjustable leather straps from each corner of the bed, and it wasn't long before Michael's arms were stretched rather wide. Ben tightened the bonds even more, and Michael was even more helpless. He couldn't even move his arms an inch. "Now put your legs together" said Ben. Michael did so, and in a heartbeat, the boxers came sliding off in an instant. All that remained was that chastity belt. The bane of Michael's existence. In less than 30 seconds, Ben slid the code to the right place and pulled – the lock opened. Michael felt a wave of joy run all over his body. Slowly, the belt slid off. It was gone. Michael nearly cried in relief. Then, of course, Ben spread Michael's legs apart and fastened them with straps very tightly. Michael was tied to a big bed, completely immobile, naked except for a hoodie. As crazy as it was, Michael felt somewhat at ease. Then, he popped a question:

"So, Ben?"

"Yes, slave?"

"Why the hoodie?"

"Well," snorted Ben, amused, "I like it because it gives you protection. A very thin, pointless protection. If I were to tickle your ribs with my fingers right now, you'd still be tickled, but that little bit of weave fabric will take a very small amount of that tickle away. You'll have the illusion of protection. When I slowly slide it up, and begin tickling your bare ribs, however, you'll feel like it's being stripped away, and you'll be even MORE vulnerable than you were before. With a tickle victim, the more you can 'build' their anxiety, the better payoff you'll receive."

"Ah… so, you're going to tickle me then."

"Heh, you're a smart one, aren't you, Michael?"

"I figured as much."

"But, my friend, you don't know HOW I'm going to tickle you, do you?"

"No, I guess I don't."

"Michael, I want to try something…"

Ben leaned over and put his mouth right to the ear of his bound friend. The first word came in, very intimate: "feet." Michael's eyes opened. "My feet." Michael felt a small tingling in his balls. And then… "I am barefoot right now." Ben wasn't, and Michael knew that (he hadn't heard the sound of any shoes plopping to the floor), but those words alone caused Michael to get a little hard. "You're horny for my *bare feet*, aren't you, Michael?" The way that Ben softly pointed the words "bare feet" was enough to send him off, and, still wearing a hoodie, Ben was spread out, naked, and with a hard cock pointing directly at the ceiling. Then Ben said the words he most dreaded: "Now we're going to have fun…"

Ben took of his Chuck Taylors but kept his ankle socks on. He sat himself between Michael's bare, exposed legs, and leaned forward. Ben's hands slowly placed a small grip on the base of Michael's hoodie. Then it came: "Tickle."

Ben's fingers slowly kneaded the lowest rib on Michael's body, and Michael – still somewhat resilient, clenched his mouth tightly. A smirk, half-giggle emerged, but Michael was going to fight it off. The fingers softly but firmly danced in a slow pattern: index middle ring pinkie index middle ring pinkie, over and over. The hands kept this pattern as they slowly moved up the hoodie, kneading the ribcage as it went along. Index middle ring pinkie index middle ring pinkie. Another half-giggle. A snort. A grunt. Michael's mouth was stretched into a horrible, Joker-like grin, but he couldn't do anything about it. He was horny, bound, and ticklish, and through his years of training, Ben knew how to push his buttons. Suddenly Ben's big index fingers jumped to Michael's nipples and began fondling and circling them. That by itself would be a torment, but because they were doing it THROUGH the red hoodie fabric, the electric sensation just increased. Michael's hardon got harder, but the waves of pleasure started coming. The nips got harder and firmer, and the more protruded they got, the more Ben played with them. Back and forth, round and round, side to side, a slight, soft tug. Michael knew he was going to go insane. And then it was hands at the ribs again: index middle ring pinkie index middle ring pinkie index middle ring pinkie index middle ring pinkie. The hands got faster, and finally the dams broke: Michael let out a chortled laugh, but couldn't even complete it, as the next wave of tickles was coming right after to muffle it.

Yes, Michael's ribcage was a tickler's delight. Ben traced each rib from side to front with his fingernails (through the hoodie, naturally), and tickled the soft spots in-between. Without warning, the hands darted under the hoodie, went right up to Michael's stretched armpits, and then clutched his sides. The index fingers began circling the little patches of armpit hair that Michael had, and they caused delightfully involuntary muscle spasms. They tickled and tickled and tickled. Sexual lightning coursed through Michael's helpless body. His hips flexed without warning. The toes wiggled in their desire to escape. Worst of all, Michael tried to bring his arms down *just a bit* to stop the tickling in his pits, but he was bound so tight he couldn't even do that, straining and laughing and convulsing all at once. Michael was fucked.

The hands came out the hood, and began tickling the ribcage right at the base of the hoodie. They moved up again, but began dragging the hoodie with it, all the way up to his neck. Michael desperately (desperately) begged a "no!!" but it wasn't going to happen: as the index middle ring pinkie motions went up his ribs, it drug that hoodie with it, and Michael was more naked and exposed than ever. "Bare ribs?!" said Ben with a joking sort of relish. "I bet they're even MORE ticklish!!" Michael screamed in anguish as Ben's too-powerful hands mined for laughs wherever they could, but unfortunately that's all he could do now: scream and laugh. Even if Michael wanted to stop doing either, the tickling, cunning hands prevented him from having any sort of free will. Ben found it beautiful.

An hour of uncontrollable laughter passed.

Ben stopped, and Michael panted in bucket breaths. Ben looked at his sweaty friend with a mixture of envy, pity, and lust. As Michael panted even more, Ben simply said "Michael… would you like some feet?"

Michael weakly yelled "More than anything sir!"

"You got it."

Ben swung his legs around, and suddenly two ankle-socked feet were near Michael's face. Michael looked at the sole of the socks: there was enough of a lightly dirty outline to tell exactly where his curves and toes were. "I've been wearing these for three days straight," Ben interjected. The feet inched closer, and, despite being bound tightly, Michael could already feel the heat from those feet hitting his face. Michael leaned in, placed his nose right at the base of Ben's left big toe, and inhaled. His cock throbbed within seconds. Michael kept on breathing in Ben's foot sweat, and with each inhale, got harder and harder. Michael, already worn down from the tickling, was just a lightning rod of pleasure. There was no filter between his brain and his cock: it was all animal right now, and all Michael wanted to do was smell. As the sniffing got more furious, Michael then used his teeth to pull off each sock, and there they stood: the mighty, meaty, just-perfectly-slightly-damp feet that he had always dreamed of. Michael smelled again, and Ben clearly saw another mighty cock-twitch. Michael liked this. Then, he looked at the left foot, and stuck out his tongue, slowly dragging it from the heel… to the arch… to the balls of the feet… and to the toes. If he was stimulated, he would've cum right then and there. More licks. More licks. Michael lived out his fantasy, and he almost cried from joy. He then finally stuck Ben's big left toe in his mouth, and sucked on it like a flesh lollipop. Back and forth, his tongue lightly tapping the toenail; Michael did so with each of Ben's toes. When Michael caught a glimpse, he saw Ben nursing his own hardon.

In the midst of all this worship, Michael's face cooking under the feeling of warm feet, Ben reached for something he had set aside on his little bedside table which Michael failed to notice when he came in. It was a rag. A soft rag. There was a bottle of oil too. Ben poured some oil into the rag. Then, he placed the small little rag right on Michael's cockhead. Michael gasped a little in the midst of a toe sucking, but continued. Slowly, Ben turned the oiled rag back… and forth… and back… and forth, like running half an orange on one of those juicing devices. Michael's pleasure-meter shot into the stratosphere. Although the oil naturally dripped down the length of Michael's cock, so did oodles of precum, all mixing together with Michael's body sweat to form a horny little cocktail on his balls and cockbase. Michael, getting off while licking some feet, was in total ecstasy. Yet… something was wrong. Ben was only working his cockhead… not the shaft at all. As pleasurable as this all was, Michael was approaching a climax… but not getting the proper nerves touched for him to cum. It was just all cockhead pleasures and footlicking… his shaft was begging, begging to be touched. After minutes of frustration, Michael stopped his foot tonguing and asked Ben:

"Hey Ben?"

"Master."

"Oh, right. Um, master?"

"Yes?"

"Could you please touch my shaft? I'm... I'm fucking horny and want to cum, sir."

"You... you want me to touch your shaft?"

"Yes sir."

"Do you mind if I touch it in... my way?"

"Um... yes sir. Just please... touch it."

Ben grabbed another item from that nightstand. Suddenly, Michael felt it – it was a big, loose, fluffy feather. There was some firmness to it, but not too much. Slowly, Ben dragged it across the top of Michael's shaft. Michael inhaled as he did so, and, as Ben's feet were close to his face, inhaled some foot sweat as he did so, which, in turn, caused his shaft to twitch (again). Then the feather did the same motion across the topside of his shaft. Then on the underside. Then Michael realized that Ben was simply sawing at his cock with a feather, tickling it as he smelled the best feet of his life. Fuck, it was too much. Another saw on his sensitive underside. Another saw on the rim of his cockhead. Another... oh fuck.

Without warning, Michael's body spasmed, and a whole months' worth of sperm buildup came flying out of his cock. Flying towards the ceiling. Then another stream, then another. Then another. Michael let out a moan of pleasure that sounded nothing short of supernatural. His body was filled with electricity. Yet for being as teased as long as he was, Michael soon began begging for his cock to stop, but it kept on cumming against his will. Michael couldn't even believe he even had this amount of cum in him. He came again, and again, and again, and it was almost hurting he was cumming so much. Finally, finally, it stopped. Michael's body collapsed, spent. Ben pulled his feet away and adjusted himself so that his mouth was right next to Michael's ear. Michael heard Ben reach for something from the nightstand and something else actually on the bed, but couldn't figure out what it was. Ben whispered in Michael's ear:

"How was that?"

Michael smiled weakly, "You are a god at what you do."

Ben continued: "So, how about this: why don't you live here with me for a while. I'll go to my job during the day, you can work on that children's book that you've been slaving over for almost a year while I'm gone, and at night, we'll eat some food, watch some movies, and have so much fun together we won't even know when to stop. How does that sound?"

"Ben, that sounds absolutely beautiful."

Ben reached over for a kiss, and got it. Michael's mouth hung open for a second... and then something was shoved in it.

Ben had attached his worn ankle socks to a gag when Michael wasn't looking, and now tied said gag around Michael's mouth. A blindfold was next. Michael tried screaming... but just gave in and suckled the sock taste for a bit, enjoying it. Then, Ben revealed a secret:

"Michael, I'm pleased you agree with me, and I know that going through a month without jacking was hard, but the day I sent you that package, I took a vow myself not to cum, and I kept it, not even cheating once. So now, while you just got off for what may actually be the 100th time to my feet, I'm going to indulge in my first cumshot based off of you. Of course, I shouldn't even have to tell you how much more sensitive a body gets after cumming... especially after a cumshot like that..."

Michael screamed into his sock gag with his last remaining strength as Ben dug his fingers into his sides. Yet even as he did so, Michael was smiling... and not just because he was being tickled...

CHAPTER TWO

THE PLEDGE

We all have those friends: those ones who we keep around somewhat for amusement more than actual friendship. It's not like we're cruel (hell, we might be someone else's social amusement), but sometimes it's just fascinating to see how these people react to the changes of life, signposts along the way. I got extremely fascinated by one such friend of mine (who has the softest of feet), and wondered: with all of his unjustified ego, selfish opinions, and holier-than-thou attitude, what would it take to shake him of these habits? Thankfully, I think I found a deviously hilarious way to do so…

Aden was about to become invisible. The best part was that he wouldn't even have to try.

Aden was your typical freshman year frat pledge. He barely turned 18, looked fit but had a slight bit of a gut when he lifted up his shirt (which he worked on every day), and short brown hair that – if combed just the right way – made him immediately look like he came out of church choir practice. Yet if Aden was good at one thing, it was believing his own hype. If there were people that could party hard, well he could prove that he could party harder. If someone was telling a funny joke, he'd tell one that he just knew in his gut was funnier. He truly felt he was cut from a different cloth, but what he didn't know was that amidst all his projections of himself as the coolest guy in the room, he was actually off-putting and frequently came off as a bit of a dick. Some wondered that even if Aden was aware of this, would he even care?

But here he was, drunk at another mixer at Tau Kappa Lambda, feeling a part of the Fraternity when, in fact, he was a pledge, just like everyone else. Aden always stood out: while the other guys were happy to add to the bro-heavy atmosphere, wearing T-shirts, cargo short and flip-flops like the rest of the known collegiate universe, Aden still wore slacks, socks with his tennis shoes, and a single button-down shirt as he always did. Tonight was another pledge mixer, and, ultimately, people were a little disappointed that Aden showed up. Some were even surprised: he had been somewhat "choosing" which pledge events to go through. Things like the ceremonies and whatnot – those meant something, and therefore he felt the need to be there. But the obstacle course? The scavenger hunt? That wasn't what it meant to be a part of a Frat. That was just stupid. He could have been expelled from consideration many times over, but Anthony was in charge of Tau Kappa Lambda and frequently gave him the benefit of the doubt – much to the chagrin of several other senior members of said Frat. Only adding fuel to their fire was Aden's behavior tonight, drunkenly belittling one sorority girl who stopped by who said she was Christian, demanding that someone else change the iPod playlist 'cos this one was boring him, and getting smacked by no less than three different girls who were in attendance for this Friday night event.

Aden was striking out, but was so drunk on booze and his own sense of entitlement that he didn't seem to notice, in his mind dismissing these girls as sluts who he didn't even want to sleep with anyways.

After getting the cold-shoulder from half the people in attendance, he stumbled his way upstairs and into the bathroom. He washed up, stepped out into the hallway of the huge frat house, and heard some strange rap song from the rooms below (were they saying "skee skee skee"?). NOW those shots from earlier were hitting him, so he stumbled unknowingly into some frat brother's room. The lights were off. No one was in there. Before he even considered lying down to recover, he tripped backwards into the room's closet, and he sat there next to some shoes and a laundry hamper. It hurt a bit, but... well, fuck, he didn't want to move now. He was strangely comfortable. He nuzzled his head against the wall of the closet, and began dozing off. With the lack of lights and his obscure position, no, no one would be able to see him even if they looked. Aden had turned temporarily invisible and he didn't even know it.

The door to the room slammed open. Aden opened his eyes – how long had it been? An hour, maybe? Either way, it was still dark in the room, but he could clearly see two guys entering the room, arms around each other, moving feverently. Were they... fighting? No, they were... kissing? Holy shit, they were kissing. Aden squinted a bit more in his haze, and noticed that the two guys were – some of the Frat members. Not pledges – full-on brothers. One of them was the dark-haired guy with Italian heritage, Jason, who was a bio major. The other was the blond, frisky Damien, a Chemistry major. Aden frequently dismissed them as eggheads, but couldn't have possibly guessed that they were gay, much less into each other. Amidst their making out – which, from his intoxicated angle, was just a furious mesh of flesh continually transmogrifying before his eyes – Jason and Damien eventually made it onto the bed. Suddenly Aden realized: this was Damien's room. He had been in here before. Suddenly, as Jason was lying down with his head on the pillow, Damien turned to him and said "May I?"

"Of course," Jason replied, with a grin. Both guys were intoxicated on *something*, but Aden just couldn't tell what it was.

While Jason lay on the bed, Damien had propped his back up against the wall, still sitting on the bed, so Jason's sneakered feet were right in his lap. He slowly ran his fingers down the seams of Jason's blue jeans, which Jason favorably responded to. Eventually, Damien's thin, devious fingers made their way down to Jason's sneakers and began… to fondle them? That's what it looked like from Aden's angle. Because they didn't turn the light on, it was hard to tell. Yet Damien was definitely feeling those sneakers with relish, his fingers darting in and out of where the laces were, eventually untying them. There was definitely a strong sexual element to what was going on – it was almost foreplay for them, Aden deduced. Then, Damien SLOWLY pulled off Jason's left shoe – and then the right. Suddenly, Jason's thick white ankle socks were exposed. Jason's socked toes wiggled with their newfound freedom, which only seemed to hypnotize Damien more. "You like that?" Jason quipped. Almost embarrassed but with a hint of excitement at the same time, Damien managed out a "Yeah…" Both grinned. Aden, as fascinated as he was somewhat repulsed, had no idea what was going to happen next…

Suddenly Damien's fingers circled the rims of Jason's socks like vultures at their pray, hooking under the rim of the elastic and teasing Jason as to what was going to happen next. Jason's face was awash with a look that said "God I'm so fucking lucky to have this happen to me", while Damien's face was saying "God I'm so fucking lucky I get to do this!" Suddenly, Damien's fingers tightened their grip around the sock, and slowly pulled it off of Jason's foot – past the heel – over the arches – and finally dangling over the toes. And with that, Jason's left foot was bare. His toes stretched a bit. Damien took the sweaty sock right up to his face and his inhaled. His whole body arched and then shuddered with pleasure, which itself put a grin on Jason's face. The routine repeated with Jason's other foot, and suddenly Damien held both socks up and got a double-whiff – he was in fucking heaven. Even though Jason's bared feet were now in Damien's lap, Jason began kneading Damien's crotch with his feet, and before long Damien was moaning in pleasure, his cock already hard as steel and straining through the blue denim it was caged in. He tried like hell to be calm, but having Jason's gorgeous, meaty size

11 feet – with such wonderfully plump toes – massaging his pleasure stick was causing him to go into overdrive (as he would later describe in a private blog post, Damien's cock was "radiating with pleasure – every single point of contact with those feet were sending pure electricity through my body – fuck I was horny"). Yet right before it looked like his body was about to go into overdrive and cum through his jeans, Damien showed restraint and stopped the foot-fuck that was happening, turning to Jason and saying, "OK, now it's time to try something on you…"

Aden was practically frozen in the closet. He didn't know what to think. However, he couldn't help but believe that somehow, he could use this to his advantage. He very quietly got out his cell phone and made sure all the screen settings were as dimmed down as possible so he wouldn't be noticed. He broke out the video feature, and began quietly filming what he saw next:

Damien got off the bed and Jason scooched down so that his bared feet were hanging just over the edge of the too-small frat mattress. Damien got on the floor and knelt down. Given the small height of the bed, by being on his knees, Damien was now facing Jason's gorgeous soles, and was in heaven. He quickly undid his pants, pulled out his coated-in-precum cock, and then placed his nose right at the base of Jason's toes. He inhaled, and Aden could clearly see Damien's cock twitch with pleasure. This was getting intense. Then, out came Damien's tongue, and it began to slowly trace the soles of Jason's feet, slightly tickling him along the way but mainly coating that boy with sweet horny pleasure. Before long, one of Damien's hands was jacking himself off furiously, and it didn't take long for Jason to join in as well. Jacking was one thing, but jacking off a pent-up, horny cock while having someone pleasure your toes, sucking on them wholesale – that was another realm altogether. It didn't take long, because both boys soon came at the exact same time, Jason's toes clenching within Damien's mouth right as Damien was sucking harder than ever. Jason's cumshot flew clear over his shoulder while Damien came hard right into the side of the bed. Both boys were motionless, the only thing moving being their chests as they panted deeply – it was intense for both of them.

Aden, meanwhile, was trying to hold his breath as best he could. He didn't want to give himself away, but he couldn't wrap his mind around what just happened. These guys got off on… feet? Smelling and licking and sucking feet? What the fuck was this? Without thinking, Damien picked himself up and crawled into bed with Jason, and both boys simply laid there, content with each other. After a few minutes, they were both snoring heavily.

Aden was ever-so-suspicious, but quietly got up and was as quiet as could be. Every creak in the floor from a sneakered footstep felt louder than a bomb, but the drunk, cum-spent, exhausted boys wouldn't have heard him even if they wanted to. Aden made it out into the hall and back to the main floor of the Frat. The music kept going, but the place was mostly empty – the party was definitely winding down, if not wound down completely. Some people were making out on the couch, the floor felt sticky from spilled beer out of cheap plastic red cups, and the place had an air of, well, an abandoned frat party. Aden made it back to his room unnoticed.

Opening the keys to his place, Aden was actually able to breathe for once, he felt. Here was his too-gorgeous single that his parents were paying out the nose for: third story of a building, glass "window wall" that gave him a nice overview of the campus (with curtains to close it all, naturally), and a nice art-deco vibe to the place. Aden particularly liked the standing bar he had. That was his favorite thing. He took off his shoes and socks and then got himself a small splash of brandy, wondered for a moment if any of the girls at the party would Facebook friend him tonight, but, alas, it was not to be. He still wondered how anyone could get off on a foot, and looked down at his own – typical build, well-kept nails, and nice meaty toes – and wondered just how anyone could like this. Oh well. He didn't think much about it. His exhaustion mixed well with his brandy, and before long, he passed out in his bed.

———————

Aden woke up around 1PM the next day (a Saturday), and got a strange message in his e-mail inbox.

It was from Jason, who was in charge of Pledge Recruitment. It basically said that after hearing about his behavior from some of the other Pledges and some of the visiting girls at the party, Tau Kappa Lambda decided that he did not have a place in the Frat, ending by wishing him luck in the coming school year. The e-mail included everyone's name in the signature, including Anthony. That last one is what stung the most.

If Aden had a glass of brandy in his hand, he'd throw it against the wall right now.

How DARE they! After attending their stupid events, going to their parties with douchebags and stuck-up girls all around and dealing with all their hypocrisy and whatnot, he had to deal with this? This was bullshit. Aden actually began pacing around his apartment in a bit of a rage, and would've broken something were it not for the fact that most of his stuff – the Japanese-only James Bond DVD box set, the cherished Disney animation cells – was actually worth money. After a bit of pacing and trying to calm down, he decided to pick up his phone and text a friend back home about this BS predicament... and then remembered something. Oh that's right... he got a video last night. A very, very incriminating video. A smirk crept its way across Aden's face. "This... this will show them not to fuck with me" he thought.

He sent back an e-mail to Jason, saying that they should reconsider kicking him out, especially after he RE:'s to the rest of the Lambda e-mail list and lets everyone see what he and Damien were doing last night. He dropped the word "fag" in a couple of times just to drive the message home. SEND.

Two minutes passed. Aden then got an e-mail back from Jason. It was pretty straightforward: "We're sorry about any misunderstanding – do you mind if we talk this over? Just you, me and Damien? Your place?" Heh, heh – they were playing RIGHT into Aden's trap, getting desperate to the point where they were willing to meet on HIS home turf. Aden simply RE'd with where his single was located, a time (8PM), and a P.S. that said that he had already made copies of the video he got (which was a lie – but they couldn't check that). Another two minutes passed before Jason responded "see you then".

Aden broke out the N64 for the rest of the day and played some Zelda games to take his mind off of the forthcoming encounter, but eventually microwaved himself some leftover pizza before 7:30PM stuck. He put on some Adult Swim reruns he DVR'd, but at 7:55PM, there was a knock at his door. There stood Jason – in a yellow Ultimate Frisbee T-shirt, cargo shorts, white ankle socks and tennis-shoes, as always – and Damien – blue-T-shirt, jeans, and a pair of cheap black Old Navy flip-flops – at the door, each carrying a grocery bag. Aden could clearly see the liquor bottles sticking out over the top. This was one hell of an olive branch they were offering – and all Aden had to do was simply catch them engage in fetish play and call them "fag". In Aden's mind, this was about as win-win a situation for him as he could get. Yet he decided to play it smooth, and simply said "Come on in…"

The boys came in and Aden directed them to the couch in front of the TV, an episode of *Aqua Teen Hunger Force* paused part-way through. They sat down and Aden sat in adjacent chair. Jason began to speak, but Aden cut him off:

"So, you guys, I know why you're here. You don't want to be embarrassed – I get it. But, seriously: kicking me out of the pledge process? That's pretty low…"

Not expecting to go on the offensive so soon, Damien casually butted in: "Aden, you got to understand where we're coming from. We don't just allow anyone who's anyone into the Frat. We all go through sacrifices and things we don't want to do. It's not a matter of enduring that stuff though – it's a matter of becoming Brothers with a capital B. There's a…"

"Yeah, yeah, yeah, I get it," Aden interrupted. "More accurately, you're backing down after I see you guys play with each other. I mean, that's kind of spineless."

Jason started, "Aden, what Damien and I do is between us, just as how what you do is between you and yourself. We don't pry, because we…"

Aden injected again: "Seriously? C'mon guys. I know the spiel. Again, you just don't want your secret exposed. Now I see you brought drinks to try and change my mind about releasing the video, so break 'em out why don't ya?"

Jason and Damien tried like hell to bite their tongues – it was hard. Yet they were civil. Damien looked around. "Mind if I use your bar?" Aden said "Go ahead." Aden liked lording over his domain. Then again, Aden liked being in control. He always did.

While Damien made some drinks (he was a part time bartender, unbeknownst to Aden, who never bothered to ask), Jason got down to business. "So, Aden, there's a reason why we're here. Obviously, we would not like the video to come out, but it's not a matter of reinstating you into the Frat just like that. Again, the girls complained last night directly to Anthony, so, really, this is bigger than the three of us…"

"What do you mean?" asked Aden. Damien was finishing up and brought over some lemony vodka mixtures that looked great in small cups.

"Well," said Jason, as Damien handed the boys their drinks, "let's say you get in. Let's say that the girls and other brothers complain about your… um, attitude. You can release the video all you want, but if Anthony still gets complaints, there's little we can do. I mean…"

"What if I say that this video represents what goes on at Tau Kappa Lambda all the time?"

Damien sat down on the couch. Jason sighed. "Aden, we're trying to extend an olive branch here. So why don't we just take a drink and start things off right, OK?" Aden smiled and said "I can drink to that." The boys clinked their glasses and took a sip.

Aden stopped for a second, and stared at his glass. "Does this taste weird to you guys?" Damien and Jason smirked. Aden was about to run in a panic, but whatever was in the drink just hit him like a hammer – and his body froze up.

Jason jumped into action and grabbed Aden's body, holding onto it gently. Damien cleared a space on the floor of Aden's apartment, and then got out a pillow right in the center. Aden's body… wouldn't move. Damien then came over and grabbed Aden's legs. The boys hoisted Aden's body onto the floor and placed his head on the pillow pulled from the couch. They put his body in an X-pattern, and then after checking his mouth, they both sat on the couch, and quietly, calmly finished their drinks.

Aden was freaking out. His body... wouldn't move. Not a finger, not a toe, not an anything. His heart, though panicked, was still beating. His lungs were still breathing. He could move his eyes and blink his eyelids if he really put his mind to it. But, that's it. He was trapped in his own body. He couldn't move a single fucking thing. What were these bastards doing to him?

"Aden," Jason started, "we're... sick of you. All of us are. The Frat brothers, the girls who stop by our parties just to have fun, and hell even people who stopped me in passing between classes to let me know that we SHOULDN'T let you into the Frat 'cos you're a dick. You're insensitive. You say stupid things and upset people. You think you're the shit when in fact you just act like a shit. People can't stand you and god help anyone who does. The straw wasn't mocking our fetish or calling us fags – although your rampant homophobia hurts us too. No, it was threatening to send your supposed video to our other Brothers. Keep in mind: they won't care – they're our Brothers. But seriously, this is how you respond to being kicked out of our Frat? By threatening us? Being in a Frat isn't about you advancing your career. No, it's about being in a team. And tonight, we're going to teach you ALL about being on a team..."

Aden tried to scream, but he couldn't.

"You see," started Damien, who Aden deduced was normally the quiet one, "we just paralyzed you. Not permanently, mind you, but being a chemist as long as I have, you learn how to cook up a few things." As Damien talked, Jason got out a pair of scissors and began snipping off Aden's shirt, pants, and boxers, much to his protest. "What we have here is targeted muscle paralysis. Your body muscles can't move, but your heart and lungs can. You're a fully-functional person except for your extremities. Your body can still feel stimuli – which we're counting on – but that's it. This is worse than the tightest bondage because you can't fight back even if you tried. Oh, and you can try like hell – we encourage you, even – but your body is OUR body for the next eight hours. And boy, are you going to enjoy the ride…"

SNIP. Suddenly, Aden was naked on his own floor in an X-pattern with only his socks on. The two guys could see his cock exposed to the world. It was beyond humiliating. The guys then began pacing around their prey very slowly.

"Aden, tonight we are going to get you to become a member of our Frat. We really are. But first, we have to get you all initiated and ready to be a real team player. We want you on our team, Aden, but it has to be OUR team. Now, you're a team player, aren't you?"

Aden tried to shake his head no, but… no avail.

"It's OK, Aden; we're going to have a fun time. But first, you'd agree that your comments were a bit out of line, weren't they?"

Aden's non-existent shaking of the head continued.

"Yeah, I thought so too. So, we're going to have some fun with you, Aden. A LOT of fun. Because you don't own sandals – as far as we can tell – and frequently dress up in long-sleeve, long-panted type outfits, I would guess you don't get much sun or rough tumbles. So, your skin must be soft… and sensitive, right?"

Aden was a bit scared, but suddenly Aden laid a very thick piece of cloth over his eyes. It wasn't attached or anything – it just lay there… and Aden couldn't see. What were they going to do to him? I mean, if they were going to…

Aden felt something. Across his leg. It was… soft. Could it have been…?

… Then another movement, across his exposed armpit. He tried to rein it in, but…he couldn't. Then another brush… across his left nipple. Did the boys break out… feathers?

OH. FUCK.

Suddenly, feathers began tracing the lines of his arms and ribs, going up and down, up and down, slowly, teasingly. It… fucking tickled. Shit! Aden was ticklish. Oh god was he ticklish. And these boys… they knew how to get him. Aden was laughing on the inside… but he couldn't fucking smile! He was trapped in a tickle chamber known as his own body! Suddenly the feathers concentrated on his pits… and they circled slowly, touching every single nerve ending. Aden's was screaming with laughter on the inside but quiet as a mouse on the outside. The feather circled the craters of his pits, tickling his hairs, and seemed to dance with an almost evil relish. They were teasing his body, and trying to break his will. Aden tried to resist... but this was getting hopeless fast.

The feathers danced around his ribs, and scraped the front of his belly, circling the base of his gut all the way to the insides of his belly button. The feathers LOVED the belly button, lapping at it with great intent. Sometimes a feather would jump back to his armpit just for variety, but tickles were being mined EVERYWHERE. Aden was just so fucking ticklish. He couldn't stand it. His rage towards them was less focused now – all his mind was filled with was tickle. Tickle, tickle, tickle. Feather, feather, tickle. Fucking hell, he was losing it.

Soon the feathers began circling the insides of his thighs. That tickled even more. Slowly, the feathers teased their way upwards, up to his exposed crotch, and then right in the gooch. Oh, the feathers had a fucking party in the gooch, circling and tickling his most sensitive of areas. Around and around and up and down. Then they circled his sensitive balls, and painted every inch of them with feathery torment. Perhaps that's what got Aden the most: not the tickling itself, but the TEASING tickles, the ALMOST tickles, the playful tickles that were having such fun and delight while he was suffering through hell. Complete hell, made of tickles and feathers.

Yet the ball tickling was upping the ante. Jason and Damien weren't as much using the edges of the feathers as much as the very very very tips of them, and they were teasing the base of Aden's cock – and, suddenly, it twitched. WHAT?! Aden's cock was twitching and moving and... slowly becoming erect. Had the potion worn off? Aden tried to move his left arm with all of his might, but nothing happened. So why was his cock suddenly coming to full HOLY SHIT A FEATHER WAS MOVING ALONG HIS SHAFT!

Aden had never felt anything like it. It felt SO fucking good! Tickled along his radiating member... it was a rush he wanted to bathe in and lean in towards, but, alas, there was nothing he could do. It was a dirty tickle: he didn't want to like it but he kind of wished they wouldn't stop. He was being manipulated by two guys, but, fuck, a girl had never made him this horny since ever. Every single feather stroke made his dick feel like it was tingling with horniness, and then the feather stroke after pushed his horniness into the next level. His mind was focused entirely on his throbbing cock right now, and a very small dribble of precum was emerging from it – and his arms still hadn't moved in some time. Or his legs. Or anything. He was motionless save for his erection.

The feathers circled and teased and tickled his cock, and then finally he wanted to cum… but he couldn't. The throb was there, but there was no push from his body. It just… throbbed. Throbbed with anticipation – but that push over the edge never, ever came. FUCK HE WANTED TO ORGASM AND FEEL SPERM SHOOTING OUT OF HIS COCK… but instead, the feathers just circled some more. And more. And were driving him bananas. Then, suddenly, Jason said "Get a whiff of this…" Jason's dirty socked foot was shoved right into Aden's nose, and Aden had no choice but to inhale. That foot funk. That odor. It was so… off-putting. Suddenly the erection subsided, much to Aden's frustration – but the foot remained there, looming over his face and teasing him. All Aden smelled was Jason foot sweat and he wanted to gag. It wasn't uber-rank or anything, but it was enough. Then Jason removed his foot, and let Aden's sweat-riddled body just lay there – motionless as before.

Then the feathers attacked the nipples, circling and tickling Aden's pleasure-centers. They teased so softly and so quietly that Aden again wanted to scream. Yet then the feathers moved to the armpits and biceps for some more feather-light tickle teasing… and then into the cavernous tickle pits again… and then to the nipples. The cycle began again.

Then the feathers stopped, and something else touched Aden – two eager tongues, descending onto his nipples. They slurped slowly, every single microscopic tongue bump dragging across Aden's nips at an incredibly slow pace. Then, the tongue flicking started across his nips. Flick after flick after flick. The boys' saliva began dripping and pooling all over them. Suddenly, Aden's dick was hard again. Then the tickling went back into his pits. Then the frustration… just escalated.

After ten more minutes of non-stop teasing, Damien went over and began lightly licking and slowly sucking on Aden's cock. Aden has had his cock sucks before – mostly by freshmen girls who didn't know any better – but fuck, Damien was a pro. Aden went immediately into that realm hovering over a brain-busting climax. The faint slurping, sucking sound in the distance only turned Aden on all the more. Jason sat down and gently put Aden's nipples between his fingers and began lightly rubbing them back and forth and back and forth. Aden – mentally exhausted – was in heaven, his body a pleasure playtoy for two horny Frat guys. Continuing the nipple teasing, Jason finally spoke:

"You know what's great about a formula that freezes all your body muscles, Aden? It freezes all of your body MUSCLES. Your cock, however, is all tissue. We can make that do whatever we want it to for as long as we want. We're going to tease and torment the bejezus out of it. You'll be spewing an endless stream of precum in anticipation, enough for a fuckin' river, my friend. Yet… there's one catch. You see, you can't climax unless you get a push from your muscles. That's how the body works. I'm a bio major, and human anatomy is one of my favorite areas of study. What we have here is a nightmare scenario. Damien can suck you off literally for hours. Your near-climax can get bigger and bigger… but it's never going to come." Jason grinned with evil glee. "Welcome to hell. Now have some feet…"

Jason's sweaty socked feet – both of them this time, with clear outlines of Jason's toes visible from where Aden was laying – were now occupying all of Aden's face. The smell was forced and unmistakable… but Damien's cocksucking was like a goddamn miracle machine, hitting every one of Aden's pleasure buttons without even trying, that warm mouth hitting every gorgeous sensitive spot it could fine. All Aden tried to focus on was the horny, not the foot smell, but as much as he tried, that foot funk was still there in his face, tormenting him. After about 10 minutes of fighting the urge to be horny while sniffing a genuine jockfoot, both Damien and Jason stopped. Aden didn't climax. Again. The erection went down. Aden's frustration knew no bounds.

———————

This process continued eight more times.

———————

It was around 4AM when it began again. Aden's nipples were almost caked with dried saliva now. The sucking on his nips began yet again. His erection almost immediately shot up after frustrated anticipation (practically screaming "give me something – ANYTHING!!"), but seeing this, Jason and Damien stopped, and awaited for Aden's frisky, ticklish cock to go down. When it did, Damien turned to Jason and said, "I think it's time." Jason agreed, and with obvious relish, Jason stuck that big sweaty socked foot of his right in Aden's face one more time.

Aden's cock immediately shot up. It was throbbing. Each inhalation drove him further up the wall. Then... Aden realized it. Jason, perhaps even knowing what Aden was thinking, said "That's right. You're one of us now." As Aden sniffed, the internal screams came back...

... He was Pavlov's dog. No wait: he was Pavlov's bitch.

They got him hard time after time, but always made sure to stick Jason's foot sweat right in his face as they did so. Given how broken his mind was after all the tickling, of course Aden's brain would start connecting foot sweat with horny. Now, it had gotten to the point where all Jason had to do with his foot was stick it in his face and Aden got instantly hard. The connection was made. Male foot sweat got him horny. And what Aden didn't know at the time was that once a foot fetish is formed in the brain, it's nearly impossible to shake. The boys had given him a taste of what teamwork was all about – he was on the team whether he liked it or not.

Suddenly, broken, battered, and humbled, Aden conceded. He knew the lesson they were trying to teach him – and he got the message. He was pulling a lot of shit over something so small, willing to humiliate his would-be brothers over placement in something as simple as a Frat. Maybe these guys WERE in the right. Even if they weren't, Aden had no idea how much longer the teasing of his sensitive skin would continue – even though it already felt like a fucking eternity.

A single tear went down his face – which Jason noticed. He pulled his socked foot away, and looked at the naked, helpless, ticklish boy in front of him. "You learned your lesson, didn't you?" Aden – still blindfolded – would've nodded in agreement if he could. "Good boy," said Jason. "Now we just have to take one quick thing for ourselves and go…"

Suddenly Aden felt a tugging on his socks. They were on the whole time. They had been sweated into the whole time. All along, they were slowly being transformed into personal fetish objects for the two devious Frat brothers. Jason and Damien slowly peeled them off Aden's moist feet, held them up to their noses while kneeling in front of Aden's immobile body, and began to jack it, moaning while they indulged in flavor of Aden foot smells. Eventually they came at the same time (how do they always do that?), spraying gobs of hot cum all over Aden's chest. Since each boy was on a different side of him, the cum streams formed a bit of an X-pattern over Aden's completely immobile chest. Fuck, even the cum streams felt ticklish, even as they slowly melted down his ribs, Aden totally unable to do anything about his liquid torture…

The boys began packing up, and Damien got some sort of drink out in the glasses. Jason simply sat down between Aden's legs and began running his fingernails up and down Aden's bared soles… and Aden – horny, helpless, and more ticklish than ever – couldn't do jack shit. The laughing inside of him was worse than before – he was almost manic. Tickle Hell, again.

Eventually Damien mumbled something about the drink being ready. Crouching down next to Aden even as Jason lightly ran his fingers over Aden's soft soles, Damien said "Aden, we know how you feel. We really do. All we can hope is that you come out of this a better person. There are consequences for your actions, and it's a shame that we had to teach you… but we only hope that something like this will only make you stronger. It is for this reason we want you a part of the Frat. We'll give you a quick drink that'll knock you out, and by the time you wake up, you'll be right as rain." There was a grin behind that last line. "Talk to us tomorrow, and think about what you want to do, OK?"

If Aden could've nodded in submission, he would've. Damien tilted his head up, a splash of a drink dribbled down Aden's too-dry throat, and before long, Aden was out like a light.

Aden woke up, groggy – but mobile. He stretched for what felt like the first time in years, and fuck it felt good. He looked around – he was still naked, but on his couch. He couldn't remember exactly how he got there. Then, he suddenly flashed back to last night, and one image after another jumped into his mind – and Aden felt that he had never been so humiliated in his life. A little bit of anger came back, but it soon faded. Those kids got him good. He groggily stepped over to his computer, loaded it up, and saw there were… friend requests on Facebook. Even after all of that, Jason and Damien were making an effort to reach out to him. Aden thought about one thing… and got out his phone. Yes, he still had that video file from the night he spotted Damien and Jason doing their thing. He opened it up, ready to upload onto his computer, but… wait. It was different. Same file name but, no… it was a shot of him getting horny at the first sniff of Jason's foot. Just like that – instantaneously. It was… degrading to even look at. He checked his phone message outbox – looks like Jason already e-mailed it to himself. For the first time in his life, Aden felt that he had gotten his comeuppance.

Maybe it was time, he thought. Maybe he HAD hurt some people before. Were… were they right? No, they couldn't be! HE was always right… or maybe Aden was just full of shit. He had never thought of himself in that way, but what if what they said was true? What if people really did complain that much? Maybe his hubris had even hurt some of his friends back home?

Aden wandered over to his bedroom to get some clothes on… and saw that Jason's dirty socks were left there on a pillow on his bed. There was a single notecard underneath that simply said "Welcome." Nothing else. Aden… no, he couldn't – or could he? Aden put his nose to the sock and inhaled. The erection returned within an instant.

After 8 hours of pent-up sexual frustration, the 15 minutes that followed were some of the happiest of his life. If only Aden knew that his adventures were just beginning…

CHAPTER THREE

THE INTRUDER

Every once in a while, you encounter someone who is far more sexual than you. One who is dominant in every way, and one who almost deliberately hunts for horny action. We know these people, we engage with them, and sometimes we even encourage their behavior. The person who I know that fits this description is someone who I've known since college who has taken his role as sexual carnivore far more seriously than you'd expect. I never engaged with him, but found his "do what I want to whoever I want" attitude fascinating, and I soon figured plugging it into a story might churn out some rather interesting results...

"That's right, sniff my toes, bitch!"

The response came in nanoseconds: "YES, MASTER!!"

Here sat Dan, at his computer, typing his subservient pleas into an IM window, horny as ever, furiously wailing away at his hardon, his work slacks tangled down at this ankles, his work shoes not even off yet. He had been on the verge of cumming for close to an hour, but the IM conversation kept getting hotter and hotter: the tip of cock was positively tingling right now – he had never been more in love with his fetish than in this very moment.

"Lick it," Jay typed.

And that's what did it.

Dan shot hard, really fucking hard, his shaft tingling through each and every moment, twitching after each propulsive shot. Beet-red from such a prolonged climax, Dan's guttural grunts of pleasure filled the room. He had cum before, he had cum over foot fetish fiction and pictures he saw online, he had even cum at the thoughts of his good friends and co-workers positively dominating him with their fresh-out-of-college bare feet, but talking to someone who was unquestionably a master at domming like this – it was a whole new experience, and it had pushed him into a state of pure animal lust. He had never felt unbridled. His body slumped in his chair, exhausted. Sweat – actual sweat! – dripped from his brow.

Jay's sent a new IM message: "How was that?"

Dan was still panting. He finally summoned up enough strength to haul his arms over to the keyboard: "Jay… I fucking owe you one after that."

"Damn right you do."

"LOL" Dan replied… even if he wasn't really laughing. He continued: "We'll have to try that for real sometime."

"Well you have to let me know when your wife isn't home, dude."

"Well," Dan started typing, and then stopped, thinking very carefully about what he was going to say next.

After all, Dan was 27 years old and had a great life out in Boston: he had a good job (accountant for a shipping firm), he had a hot wife (Aly, who was a legal clerk), and even managed to rummage up enough cash to buy a small house right outside of downtown. Yet even with all of this – he wasn't *completely* happy.

There was still a part of him that hadn't been fully satisfied. For you see, Dan had a raging male foot fetish. It was… intense, to say the least. Seeing a guy's bare toes out in the open wasn't really the basis of it (although he did appreciate a good pair of clean, plump toes that could potentially be sucked on) – it was deeper than that. What he found hot was the reason why a guy would go barefoot in the first place. Some guys were shy about showing their feet (for some inexplicable reason). Some couldn't have given less of a fuck about shoes. Others just enjoyed lounging, casual enough to wear flip-flops in the day but still wear shoes and socks to class. The mindset a guy had to be in: the openness, the implied vulnerability – in essence, the way the male ego manifested itself in everyday dress. A guy walking into Dan's frat with soccer cleats and ankle socks didn't really intrigue Dan that much. But a brother standing out on the porch of their fraternity, smoking a bowl of weed in an unbuttoned button-down shirt, pajama pants, and nothing else – it was images like that that worked Dan's imagination.

He liked the shape of a guy's toes, the length of them, whether or not they had a wisp of hair on the tops of them, how wrinkled (or dirty) the soles in question were – there were many factors. Would he like to wrap his moist mouth around a guy's bared toes and suck on them just for the experience, the taste, and the flavor? Of course. But, really, Dan was more curious about what the guy's reaction would be. He wouldn't want it to lead to more sex – that, for him, was a bit out of the question in his mind – but would the guy react favorably? Would he himself get hard? What if it was the straightest of straight guys? Could such an encounter cause wood to spring?

Dan's mind tormented him daily with these endless questions. Although he loved Aly dearly (ever since that goofy lil' college prom they went to sophomore year), his male foot fetish had been developing since high school. Joining a frat made sense to him both academically and career-wise – but one of the lingering, secret reasons he joined in the first place was because he really, really wanted to be around the bared feet of some of his collegiate peers – and that's exactly what happened. He never was bold enough to go out and actually ask a guy if he could sniff his feet or even give a foot massage – such overtures he knew would be greeted with skepticism, perhaps even dismissal. But he still swiped guys' sweaty socks out of laundry hampers when no one was around for jerking purposes. During his Junior year, he even stayed at the Frat over winter-break, and spent hours on end indulging his access to people's closets, grabbing the most sweatblackened pairs of flip-flops he could find and licking them for what felt like hours. He had outlets for his fetish – but never proper follow-ups. As such his fetish didn't develop: it sat intensifying in its adolescent stage, soon swelling to the point where he was afraid to ask anyone for time to "explore". The more potent it got, the more unsatisfied he ultimately was.

Only a few weeks ago did he reconnect with Jay, a frat brother of his who had only recently moved to Boston to work as a low-level manager for a coffee chain. It seemed strange, but Dan was happy for Jay. He was two classes behind Dan, and only after Dan had graduated did Jay actually come out as gay to his brothers – leading to many hilarious misadventures (which were, of course, communicated to Dan through the magical powers of alumni gossip). Dan honestly didn't think much of the tales, but when he saw Jay online on Facebook not too long ago, he felt like dropping a line. Suddenly they were talking on a fairly regular basis – and Jay was quite the flirt. And not the desperate, awkward kind of flirt either: in-between the last year that Dan saw him and right now, Jay must have had many, many experiences, because he was a goddamn master sexual conversationalist. Only one week after reconnecting did Jay manage to extract from Dan his secret foot fetish. Jay tossed fantasy scenarios at him again and again and again. Once Jay even sent a letter to Dan's place featuring a few pages of dirty fetish-related text that he had penned (in sending the letter to Dan's name only, he was able to side-step any possible interference from Aly). It was almost as if Jay and Dan were harboring a "special", secret relationship.

Jay's motives, meanwhile, were far more devious. Although he was living out in Boston with his boyfriend of three years, Jay wasn't merely up for going to the gay area of town and getting as much free cock as he could handle. For him, that was too easy – there was no effort involved! He had learned every possible trick and twist there was to male-male bedroom play, so once he conquered that domain, he set his sights towards more lofty goals: to seduce "straight" guys. The word "straight" always appeared in quotes in his mind, because according to Jay, no one in the world is ever 100% straight. Sure, people may not ever act on their impulses, much less talk about them, but some form of deviation is always there – Jay made it his job to distract it. He didn't just want to convince a horny frat brother to drop his pants for a free blow job, no. He wanted to make a straight guy *fall in love with him*. He wanted to bat some eyelashes and break a heart from across the room. He wanted to seduce, and by playing coy and innocent (since everyone loved the innocent ones), he was able to entice from far away. He had already pulled off that trick three times, once even getting the Treasurer of his Frat to, waking up with him one fateful Saturday morning, beg him for a kiss, for a shot at a relationship, despite the fact that he was already dating one of the best-looking Varsity cheerleaders on campus. Jay, of course, giddily denied his request. He had conquered a new mountain, and was now eagerly searching for the next one.

With Dan, he found his next challenge.

The text marker was flashing at the two young men, several miles apart in the same city. Here was Dan, exploring new horizons in himself, and here was Jay, never having met anyone with a foot fetish but wanting to give it a shot if just not to chase after his own goal: to now break up a marriage. Dan got up the strength and finished typing:

"Well, she's gone on a church retreat this weekend." Fuck, what was he doing?

A wicked grimace spread across Jay's face. The fly was now coming to the spider. "See you then, boy." Jay immediately logged off. Dan was both shocked and excited by their exchange. The gears of fate were now in motion…

————————

Friday's day shift was finally over, and it couldn't have come too soon. All throughout the week, that conversation that he had with Jay was echoing throughout his head, every moment of it. With Jay, a wild Pandora's Box of devious pleasures could be unleashed, but at what cost? Why the hell did he even tell Jay that Aly was going to be out of town this weekend? And – above all – what the hell did Jay mean when he said "See you then, boy"? Being called "boy" like that – it was a new experience for him, but Dan kind of liked it. He wondered what it would be like to worship a true foot master – but these thoughts were still firmly rooted in fantasy. The actual reality of it all terrified him. To the core, even.

The second that Dan got home, he saw a note attached to the fridge: it was from Aly, saying she left a couple of prepared meals in the freezer in case he gets hungry that evening. Dan sighed sweetly upon reading it: Aly was always doing sweet little gestures like that to just make his day a little bit brighter. Yet as Dan's mind labored on the thought, it drifted towards the computer, dragging him along with it. He just… had to login and see if Jay was online. He felt terrible that this, above everything, was his first impulse, and in cases like this, sex was trumping love. And BOY was it trumping.

Not even changed out of his work clothes, he got online, and there was Jay's profile name just winking at him, tempting him, waiting for him. Dan took some time to compose himself, and then made the initiative:

"Hey."

Jay responded with a winking emoticon. He was obviously in a playful mood. Dan then received the ominous message, "So… is tonight the night?"

Dan was doing his best at being playful in return: "The night for what?"

"The night when you finally meet a true foot master, bitch."

"Heh, heh, you're such a tease."

"It's not a tease if I mean it…"

"Heh, heh," was all Dan could muster back.

"Tonight, you're going to lick my bare, sexy soles, Dan. And you're going to love it." Jay was going for the kill.

Dan felt a bit uneasy about the whole thing. Yes, the idea of "serving" the feet of a guy seemed right up his alley, but... this was all happening too quickly, too soon. I mean, he has never had any sort of "direct" contact with the bare soles of a guy like that before, and he really, really wanted to experience that... but, now? While his wife was out of town? He felt like he was cheating in some way or another. Hell, the pangs of guilt that he felt each and every time he got a hard on thinking about feet were enough to make him swear off the whole thing. Yet, tonight, it really did feel as if he was going too far.

"Jay, I'm having second thoughts about the whole thing. I'm sorry, but I just feel weird about doing this while Aly is out of town. You know what I mean? I don't mean to give your hopes up, but... yeah."

The text cursor flashed at him. Once, twice, three times... ten times. Twenty. Nothing. Fuck, Dan thought, he screwed it up again. A golden opportunity just slipped through his fingers. He had never felt so bad about doing the right thing.

"See you soon," Jay typed back. Then he signed off.

Dan's eyes went wide. What the hell was he doing? What just happened? Dan suddenly felt a bit... panicked. Was Jay planning something? Dan stepped back from his computer. This was... scary. He was actually, genuinely scared. He jumped back and checked Facebook to see if Jay had posted anything – but nothing.

But wait – how would Jay even know where he lived even if he was planning something? Then it dawned on him: the letter that Jay sent with that story he wrote. It's not necessarily that he wanted to send him a story – he wanted his address. Dan realized that this trap had been set WAY in advance.

Dan spent close to a half hour nervously pacing around his house. He didn't know what to do. He didn't have Jay's number at all to call to figure out what was happening, but...

Ding-dong.

Dan didn't even have to guess: he knew Jay had arrived.

Nervously, Dan walked to the door. He leaned up against it and asked simply, without emotion, "Who is it?"

Jay's voice rang loud and clear from the other side: "Open the door, bitch."

So forward. So direct. Without even thinking, Dan obliged. He opened the door and Jay simply walked in like he owned the place, not even saying a word. He was dressed rather plainly: a striped blue shirt, blue jeans, and what appeared to be white ankle socks and tennis shoes. Jay had a messenger bag around his shoulder that complimented his longer, blonde hair, but right now, Jay looked more like a homeowner, with Dan as the confused guest.

Jay walked right into the living room, and set his messenger bag down next to the couch. He propped his sneakered feet right up on the coffee table, and simply stared at Dan, who had just finished locking the front door. His feet gently rocked back and forth. Dan was still speechless, and staring, blankly.

"Well what are you waiting for? Take 'em off."

Dan was already intrigued by the circle that Jay's toes were drawing in the air, but still tried his best to keep his reason above water, and mustered what he could for a sentence: "Jay, I don't know what you're…"

"Take 'em off, slave!"

The urge won. Suddenly, Dan was acting as if he was under the control of something else; some horny lust demon had overtaken his body. He walked over to the opposite end of the coffee table, and kneeled. He was now staring directly at the soles of Jay's tennis shoes, the kind with all the ridiculously complex patterns and logos on the bottom, great for advertising in snow imprints and little else. Dan, still in a state of half-shock, looked into Jay's blue eyes, and saw something that he couldn't quite place his finger on. Something that he knew he had to obey, lest there be terrible, terrible consequences.

"What are you waiting for?"

Even with everything happening at once, Dan reached out and placed his hands on the tops of Jay's sneakers. He certainly didn't have any sort of shoe-related fetish specifically, but to feel those laces, to know that those feet he was pining for were a half-inch of material away – it was enough to give him a rush. Slowly, he snuck his fingers into the knots at the top and slowly began to untie them; undoing the knots so that the laces just flapped on to the sides. "Good boy," said Jay, pleased with the progress of his young pupil. Once both sneakers were unlaced, Dan held onto Jay's left sneaker tightly so that Jay could slowly drag his socked foot out. Dan was entranced as he saw each little stitch of fabric pass by, teasing him the whole way through. The right foot followed.

Soon, two sneakers lay on the ground on either side of the coffee table. Now, as Dan sat there on the floor, two pairs of socked Jay's feet were staring back at him. He could clearly see a bit of dirt and sweat had accumulated on the bottom of the foot. Jay crunched his toes a bit just to see what sort of reaction they'd get, and Dan subconsciously leaned in a bit more, almost hypnotized by their movements. As of right now, Dan was in uncharted waters, but fuck if he hadn't been more intrigued by the direction he was heading.

"Lean in," Jay commanded. Dan did so, using his arms to prop himself up a bit. Jay then put those ankle-socked feet right on top of his head and pushed it down so that his chin was leveled flat with the table. Then, Jay moved his feet around so both soles were right up in Dan's face, canvassing it like a mask.

Then all Jay had to do was say one word: "Sniff."

Dan inhaled, and his hardon went from curious to engorged. He wore that sockmask with pride and each breath in was a validation as to why his fetish was so great. The tastes, the flavors, the smells. Heaving, heaving, heaving, suddenly Dan was almost in a new realm of pleasure. His cockhead had never tingled with so much pleasure, as a big ridiculous smile spread across his face, the corners of his mouth lightly scraping the socks in front of him as he did so.

The more he inhaled, the more Jay was encouraged to keep up this course of action. Jay took away his right foot, leaving Dan there simply to sniff all he could out of the left. The right foot then began rubbing itself over Dan's head, pushing his hair back in a comforting gesture, accompanied by a few token iterations of "Good boy!" Each time that socked wonder pet Dan's head from his forehead back, he truly felt as if he was doing a good thing, as if he was serving his function, and best of all, making his Master happy.

Wait a second: Master? Did he really just think of Jay in the context of "Master"? Holy shit. His brain was two steps ahead of him. His mind wasn't even resisting: it was lying down and letting Jay literally walk all over it, only to thank him for doing so. Each discovery that Dan had was as pleasurable as it was terrifying. He had never felt the level of satisfaction that he had while sniffing those socked feet, trumping even sex with his wife. But that nagging guilt still weighed on him, making him second-guess each and every nanosecond of this experience.

Jay spoke again: "Teeth." Dan stared at him, eyebrow arched. "Um… what?" "Use your teeth," he said, wiggling his toes, "now!"

No further explanation was needed: Dan's head craned in between Jay's feet, and placed his nose right at the elastic rim of Jay's right sock. He sniffed a bit, and could already feel a bit of sweat forming down along the heels of those magnificent feet (Dan wasn't really great at guessing these kinds of things, but if he had to, he'd estimate Jay's were a size 12). Then he moved forward a bit, and chomped the elastic rim, already caked with a bit of that tasty, salty sweat. Very slowly, he pulled the elastic rim downward, over the heel, over the soles, across the base of the toes, and then finally, it was off. Dan was there, kneeling in front of his coffee table with a worn ankle sock hanging out of the corner of his mouth, and there was Jay, laying on the futon happy as a clam, one foot socked and one foot bare. It would be obvious to anyone who walked in to know who was in control.

With the taste of captured foot sweat slowly draining into his mouth, Dan wasn't necessarily conscious to his actions or what was going on: his brain was simply suspended in the moment. All he saw before him wasn't necessarily objects of desire, not necessarily something that he wanted, but some*body* that he wanted. Perhaps he didn't know it yet, and perhaps he didn't even fully realize it, but the want, the need to please somebody wasn't there. As he was discovering, his fetish wasn't separate from anything: feet by itself wouldn't just do it for him. It was the feet of that specific individual that he was intrigued by, almost as much as the individual itself. His brain had already made this connection, although he himself had yet to realize it.

Jay was now cruelly toying with his prey. He wiggled his toes; he curled them together and slowly released them. He scratched one foot with the other, and watched Dan's eyes following each movement the whole time. The boy was hypnotized, and would obey Jay's every command. Jay decided to implement a test to see if his new slave was fully trained. He removed his feet from the coffee table and planted them firmly on the carpeted floor.

"Crawl!" he commanded.

The sock dropped out of Dan's mouth. Without thinking, he pressed his head to the floor and slowly moved his way towards his Master's feet. There they were: jeans draped over the tops, carpet pressed under the bottom. This fabric sandwich did wonders for Dan. Calling it a visual feast would be an understatement.

"Kiss them."

Dan looked up to lock with Jay's eyes, which were unflinching – this was serious. Very serious.

Dan immediately took his face to the tops of Jay's foot and started kissing them sweetly, softly. He kissed the tops, the base of the toes, the actual toenails, the tips, the spaces in-between. Everywhere. It felt good to give Master acknowledgement of his greatness, to physically give praise to his perfect, sexy feet. The physical act of kissing them only engrained the fetish deeper into his being: with each kiss, he loved doing it even more.

"OK, stop!" commanded Jay. Dan looked up. "Stand." Dan did so. Jay then stood up and saw the nervous, horny, obedient man standing before him. Jay looked him over, noticing the quickness of Jay's breath. The boy was nervous – but he had dealt with these things before. Jay began pacing the room as Dan stood, firmly planted.

"Shoes off." Dan looked at Jay, and again saw that unwavering glare of authority. He sat on the couch and began undoing his laces, soon toeing off his shoes, leaving just black works socks remaining.

"Socks off." Well, that was pretty self-explanatory.

"Now stand." Dan stood up, still in his button-down and slacks from work (he never even thought of changing for some reason), his own bare feet finding solid carpet ground to stand firm on.

Silence.

Jay slowly circled his willing victim, eyeing him even more carefully than before. He planted himself squarely in front of Dan, and grinned. Jay then started unbuttoning the front of Dan's shirt. Dan started to mouth a protest, but nothing came of it. His white undershirt was now exposed.

"Bare-chested. Now."

Dan obliged.

Dan was shedding clothes faster than he ever thought possible. Jay then grabbed the front of Dan's pants, and felt the throbbing, curious erection inside. He stroked the shaft briefly through the fabric, and Dan's reaction was a mix of surprise, disgust, and utter delight. It's like his brain had shut off completely: he was now doing only what his cock wanted and boy did it like what was happening.

Jay undid the button on the front of the pants, and then started slowly unzipping them, before yanking them down. Dan's eyes remained closed in a state of shocked pleasure as this happened. Now, with pants around his ankles, Dan stood there with a pair of boxer shorts and one muscle wanting to escape its fabric cage – *badly*. This was a rather intoxicating mix of both pleasure and pure humiliation, no doubt evidenced by the fact that a circle of precum was gradually widening on the front of his boxers.

"Meet me in your bedroom."

Dan stared back at Jay – that… that was a command?

"Now, bitch!" roared Jay. Dan was taken back quite a bit: Master was yelling at him. Dan, so easily slipping into this clearly-defined role, was terrified. He briskly walked towards his own bedroom, noticing Jay pulling something out of messenger bag as he did.

Dan stood at the edge of his bed. His own bed that he slept in with Aly every night. The slatted header and footer, its shiny wooden finish. And yet, here was someone who was about to come in and do something to him on it. Or, maybe, force him to do something to Master? Maybe this was a bad idea; after all, he was kind of...

"Face me."

Jay burst into the room, wearing the same thing as before except now he put his ankle socks back on. Dan stood at attention, as if in boot camp. He awaited orders.

Jay walked up to him and without saying a word put a blindfold on over his head. The world was engulfed in darkness. Then...

Oh, that moist, moist sucking.

Dan's mouth was agape, quivering with new pleasure. Jay was sucking Dan's throbbing cock *through* the boxer fabric, and it was a damn, sloppy, wondrous world of total pleasure. Dan already felt like he was on the verge of cumming harder than he ever had before.

Then it stopped just as suddenly as it started. Dan heard Jay rummage for something he brought into the room with him, and then felt a big leather strap get attached to his ankle, then pulled taught. Then the other ankle. Then each wrist. With the wrists in particular he could suddenly feel the true weight of these things – they were fuckin' industrial. He heard Jay move to the other end of the bed, and then...

YANK!

Suddenly Jay's arms were pulled backwards, flinging the rest of his body onto the bed. His right arm was pulled violently rigid, as if he was being dragged by a supernatural force. Then, it dawned on him: attached to each cuff was a long strap, which, when Jay pulled on them, suddenly turned Dan into a sexual marionette, awaiting the puppeteers command. Jay fastened one arm to the bed, then the other: the arms were tied to opposite ends of the headboard. Jay toyed with Dan's legs though, giving them playful yanks here and there, making him merely think he was being dragged into final position. But if only Dan knew what Jay had in mind. Jay wasn't merely going to tie Dan's legs to the ends of the footboard: that would make too small an "X". Instead, he pulled the strap to Dan's left leg much father up, moving up the actual bed itself, finding a way to tie the end to the bedspring frame underneath the mattress. Dan's legs were awkwardly skewed leftwards because of this. But then Jay proceeded to grab the right leg strap and pull that helpless little leg well to the opposite direction. It kind of hurt a bit, this stretching, as suddenly Dan's legs were spread wide. Real fuckin' wide. Suddenly, it dawned on Dan why Jay wanted to secure him this way: to have full access to his cock and balls, without anything getting in the way.

Dan then realized that he was fucked.

Unable to move a single muscle, blinded by the heavy eye pad, a hardon straining through the boxers up to the point where the fabric was rubbing against his cockhead gently enough to start driving him horny-mad, Dan was completely unsure of what to feel right now. He was fuckin' horny, yes, but not as much for feet at this moment. Being manhandled like this… that… that was a new sensation for him. He was excited and terrified at the exact same moment, but was resigned to his fate: Jay was controlling his body right now – not him.

Dan felt Jay stand on the bed, causing the mattress to depress on either side of his ribs. Then… nothing. Dan's body was tense – tenser than it's ever been! – but nothing was happening. The anticipation of the moment, the wondering of what the hell was going to happen next, possibly at any second – it was too much. Dan's almost-nude body was practically quivering in fear. This was getting intense.

Suddenly, across his nipple, he felt it: a fabric stroke. It… it was… a sock? Yes, Jay's socked foot was slowly running along Dan's ribcage, and he could feel literally every fiber of it. His cock twitched in approval. Jay was really utilizing Dan's fetish to the extreme, and figured the only way to do this was to torment him further. The toes wiggled into Dan's ribs a bit as it did, and Dan tried his best to contain his giggles. Had his blindfold been off, he would've seen Jay's mouth morph into an evil, twisted grin of delight.

Jay then took his other socked foot and began circling his big toe portion around Dan's lips, never dipping in, but teasing the boy relentlessly. He then placed the base of his toes right on Dan's nose, forcing him to inhale even more foot smell than before. The foot went on to brush across his forehead, stroke his eyebrows, and even trace his neckline. It was all utter torment for the horny fetish-boy underneath those gorgeous, perfect feet.

"Would you like my socks, boy?" Jay asked in a very seductively menacing voice.

Instead of verbalizing a response, Dan simply nodded yes very rapidly – there was absolutely *nothing* he wanted more at that exact moment. Jay placed the toe portion of his right sock right onto Jay's lips, instructed him to clench down on the fabric-y tip, and then slowly started to take his foot out of it. Off it had slipped, and soon the sock dropped down into Dan's horny mouth. Dan's tongue was bathed in flavor, and gods was he content. The routine repeated with Jay's other sock, but this time Jay took an even longer time to take his foot out of the sock: he really wanted to see how badly Dan wanted to have these things shoved in there. With that, Jay was barefoot again, and yet another sock had slapped back into Dan's mouth. Dan felt Jay get off of the bed to grab something, and then resumed his standing position over him. Dan heard the opening rip of duct-tape, but before he had any time to object, Jay placed a giant piece of it over Dan's mouth, gagging his slave completely, lodging the sweaty Jay's socks in there permanently. In Jay's mind, there now wouldn't be any problems going forward.

Suddenly Jay dropped down on the bed to a kneel, with Dan's bound body underneath him, his ribcage trapped right in-between Jay's thighs. Dan gasped in panic, stunned, while Jay started wiggling his fingers in the air. He then said three of the most terrifying words in all of the English language:

"Are you ticklish?"

Through the socks and duct tape, Dan let out as mighty a scream as he could. But it didn't manner: Jay's fingers dug into Dan's armpits, and began lightly scratching the interior of those sexy, nearly-hairless man pits. The fingernails scraped the tops of each and every nerve ending, and Dan's body tried its best to bring its arms down, to raise it's the ribcage up – just *anything* to hide his pits from the terrible tickle terror that was being inflicted on him. Dan began laughing hard – well as hard as he could with two slightly-dirty ankle socks taped into his mouth, gagging on foot sweat every few seconds.

Yet the tickles didn't stop: the fingers were relentless, and Dan was tied so tight that he couldn't even flinch an inch. The armpits were stuck there, and all they could do was just be tickled. It was pure torture for Dan – although his hardon didn't shrink.

After about ten minutes of this, Jay stopped, and got off of the bed. He grabbed something yet again, and Dan was sweating like hell. He was taking bucket breaths through his nose, trying his best to regain his composure. Then he felt Jay get back on the bed, and sat down right in-between Dan's bound legs. Jay's own legs, however, were positioned so that his toes were right in Dan's armpits. The toes slowly moved back and forth, back and forth in those pits, barely tickling them but constantly teasing Dan's fragile, horny young mind. All Jay was doing was sitting on the bed and wiggling his toes in Dan's bound, helpless pits, and the remaining strength in Dan's body was doing all it could to prevent it. A delirious, exhausting mixture of choked laughter and as good as a cock tease as he's ever experienced. Dan was hating and loving every visceral minute of it.

Jay kept this up for about five minutes, watching Dan's cock pulsate and twitch against its will, positively straining against its boxer fabric. Jay, being devious, proceeded to grab the stretched-out bits of fabric near the base of Dan's cock on each side, and then proceeded to slide them back and forth, back and forth, and ever-so-slowly. Even though the fabric near his cockhead was soaked in pre-cum, that annoying and fibery drag across Dan's too-sensitive head was driving him mad. He literally didn't know if he could stand another second – if there was a safe word he could scream he would – but absolutely nothing was coming out of his mouth in-between the screams of sexual anguish and too-deep laughter. Throughout all of this, his pitch was slowly shifting from guttural to high – high as in desperate and whiny. Right now, Dan was being owned.

Jay then broke out a pair of scissors that he had with him (they were the kindergarten kind with the rounded tips, just so no accidents would happen), and slowly began snipping away at Dan's boxer fabric. As the last cut was made, the elastic broke loose and Dan's cock was freed: entrenched with fresh air, no longer straining against the fabric, it was practically singing with delight. Yet this moment of joy didn't last too long: Jay's toes continued to tease Dan's pits again and again, causing as much squirming as the restraints would allow. If the duct-tape wasn't over his mouth, one could see Dan's mouth distorted into an unwilling smile, backed by roughly a thousand watts of tickle-energy. Dan's mind had completely lost track of time: as far it was concerned, every passing second felt like an hour of tickle hell.

Jay watched his prey whither, watched that engorged cock continue to swell, and watched the energy get slowly drained out of Dan's body. Finally, Jay determined it was time to really, really play with his victim. Out came his finely-tuned feather, and slowly, he wiggled it underneath Dan's balls. Shocked, Dan's cock strained upwards and he tried to pull his legs in, but the leg restraints were so tight and his stance so wide that all his balls could do was just dangle there, helplessly; torturous ornaments being fondled by a devious, dexterous feather that attacked Dan's nerves with laser precision.

The feather traced the crevices in Dan's ball-skin. It danced lightly around his gooch (it really liked that, staying there for a whole ten minutes). It traced along the inside of his thigh, and then lightly licked the base Dan's cock. It slowly went up that cock, feathering and feathering and feathering away, slowly up towards the midway point, past it, right underneath the rim of the head, circling the rim…

Underneath, Dan was screaming bloody murder.

Jay then placed his bare feet right on Dan's face and said "Inhale!" Dan did so, his back arched, and the feather circled the desperate, sensitive cockhead rapidly.

Ka-ching.

Dan's cock exploded, firing out rockets of cum from sheer, unbridled sexual pleasure. Foot funk in his nose, tickles electrifying his cock, hours and hours of unreleased cum buildup behind him – it was a perfect storm. One rocket fired up his chest after another, ribbons of it flying through the air. Dan was almost in tears it felt so good. But after the third or fourth stream, he thought he was done, but no – it kept on pumping against his will. More and more and more and more it went, each pump making his entire shaft infinitely more sensitive. Now it was *too* sensitive, and each pump was killing him. Yet it didn't stop: it's like he was on an endless cum cycle, and his cock just wasn't listening to reason. The tears of reluctant ecstasy were moistening the blindfold, and then, finally, the cock calmed down. Jay got off of the bed, and Dan, with barely any energy left, laid there exhausted and whittled down to nothing. Jay walked over and ripped off the duct tape over Dan's mouth and retrieved the now-chewed socks that were in there. Dan lapped the air. Jay went into Dan's fridge and got out a bottle of water so that he could replenish the strength of his little victim. Dan's eager mouth sucked down the whole bottle in nothing flat.

And then, nothing.

Dan's muscles ached like hell, and his voice was so hoarse he could barely speak. Yet he just… laid there. He felt absolutely nothing. At all. Minutes passed, and Dan's mind was scrambling to put together a timeline of events about what just happened. But where was Jay? What was going on? More minutes ticked away, and Dan was now starting to get nervous.

Suddenly, he felt Jay sit down on the side of the bed – but what was he doing?

Dan felt one of Jay's gorgeous bare feet start tracing his neckline, then move down across his chest, the toes fondling the nipples as they could. Then a second foot joined in, and soon both of Jay's feet were mashing up Dan's face, wiggling a toe in an ear, moving a sweaty sole across his mouth, and soon pushing off Dan's blindfold.

For Dan, each movement of the foot felt incredible. To have those feet touching his skin made him feel good, special even, as *he* was the one that was selected to serve these pristine flesh beauties. As Dan's mouth started subconsciously reaching out for a toe to suck on, to taste, there was a stirring. Against all odds, Dan's cock was coming back to life. First a faint tingle, then a twitch, and then a slow, gradual rising action. Dan knew he couldn't take any more, and tried filling his mind with images other than feet, but as shattered and broken as he was, it didn't really matter: Jay's feet were trumping all, and the warmth that radiated off of them was enough to make Dan want to fuck the living hell out of them. Dan was a slave of his own fetish, which was exactly what Jay was counting on.

As the cock was finally getting close to fully erect, Jay's hand soon descended and began pumping Dan's manhood firmly, getting the process going and bringing Dan to full attention in no-time. The feet were still mashing Dan's face, and Dan didn't really have any energy left to put up a fight: he was still a puppet for Jay's amusement.

Then, without warning, Jay's mouth descended on Dan's cock, and began slurping away. Jay was a pro, and knew every twist, lick, and sound that could be made to bring Dan to a climax. Dan's hips unconsciously thrust as far as they could in the warm, moist realm that was Jay's talented mouth. Pulling his mouth off, Jay instructed "Lick!" and Dan did it with a fury, madly sticking out his tongue to try and get a taste of whatever soles, toes, or tops were coming his way. Jay's mouth went in again, and Dan's sensitivity went up a notch. Jay expertly twisted and slurped, and in no time at all, Dan screamed out "Nooooo! I'm going to cum!" "I know," said Jay in devious response. Mere seconds passed, and soon Jay was sucking Dan dry of his seed, Dan blathering incoherently as his sensitivity skyrocketed yet again – it was all too much.

Jay separated his mouth again, and looked at his trembling prey. He quickly tickled Dan's balls and a yelp came out. "Please!" pleaded Dan, desperate. "Please let me go!"

"You didn't do a good job licking my feet this last time, slave."

"I'LL DO BETTER I PROMISE!"

"See," started Jay, "you've come twice in twelve minutes. Want to see if we can get you to cum four more times before the hour is up? I still think you got some cum you've been hiding from me…"

Dan was about to protest, but Jay started again, getting Dan to finish.

And again.

And again.

And again.

Dan was about to pass out at any moment, the breeze from the air in the room immediately causing his cock to shudder from oversensitivity. His face was positively caked with tears. Jay walked over and began releasing Dan from his bonds. Dan couldn't even reflexively coil into the fetal position he was so spent. Jay then sat on the bed and turned to Dan, saying simply: "Aly doesn't come back until Sunday, right?" If Dan could've screamed, he would've right then and there. Jay then added one other caveat: "Let's see if we can't get you to say that you love me – and mean it – before she returns…"

Dan wasn't sure if that revelation was the best or worst thing he had ever heard. As he discovered the next morning however, what he thought didn't really matter anymore…

CHAPTER FOUR

THE WAGER

I've been obsessing over my best friend's feet for some time. Then again, whoever my best friend is at any given moment tends to usually be an object of unrequited lust – you know how it goes. This particular one has inspired more than one story in this book (well, that's if you count this one and an earlier one), and his sandaled feet are nothing short of fantastic. Yet, when it came to using his personality for inspiration, I couldn't really write a story about it, much less an overtly horny/sexual one – that struck a bit too close to home, and overtly sexual stuff wasn't something I really wanted to do in the first place. Yet after the previous holiday season, I received a smart phone, one which allowed me to write and send e-mails to myself. So, while delayed in a Denver airport on my way home, I wrote a "quickie" of a tale that summed up everything I wanted to do to said friend, and did it all on the smallest keyboard you can possibly imagine. Thankfully, I can now pen things even when not near a computer, which joyously means that when inspiration strikes, I can follow it at any time of day, like I did here…

"I'm broke, man."

"I know."

"I… really feel bad about this, dude."

"Eric, listen to me: it happens. Sometimes you're up, sometimes you're down, but we always make it through. This time is no different."

"So…" Eric typed, knowing full well what was going to happen next, just as I did. This wasn't rocket science: Eric needed his best friend to give him money so that he's not late on his rent. Unfortunately, this wasn't the first time it happened, and although Eric did eventually pay me back before, it was nearly five months after the fact. He really, really sucked at finances. I merely watched that IM box, awaiting the creative way he'd spin this latest act of begging.

"Think I can borrow some money?"

I sighed. "Eric, I'd love to, but you know what happened before. I can't wait 5 months for you to pay me back. I mean, how much do you need this time?"

"About $80."

"You can't wait until next payday for this one?"

"Not when my rent is due in two days. Listen, I feel terrible about asking you but you're pretty much my last hope."

"I don't know," I typed back, genuinely unsure of what to do in this case.

There was a pause, and then Eric typed an interesting reply: "Maybe I can do something for you."

"What'd you have in mind?"

"Well – and keep in mind that I really hate that I'm reduced to this – perhaps I can do something foot-related."

My body shot to attention. My first thoughts were FUCK. YES. You see, Eric knew full well about my fetishes, yet – being good friends – I never acted on them. Still, that didn't prevent me from obsessing over his gorgeous, gorgeous feet. About size 10, good medium-length toes – all fit in well with his slender, pencil-frame. He had previously informed me that he's a ticklish motherfucker, and the very idea of a toothbrush being dragged across his soles made him cringe. That very idea, however, made me salivate.

My mind deviously churned for a moment, and then a ridiculously devious idea graced my mind.

"Eric, I can do you one better: how about we do a bit of a wager. An endurance challenge, if you will, that'll involve both your feet and a little bit of tickling. If you pass, you get to KEEP the money, no strings attached. How does that sound?"

"... and if I lose?"

My typed reply was eloquently simple: ">:)"

I waited patiently, smirking.

"Tonight?" He typed, knowing full well this was his last hope.

"Whenever you can make it over."

Another pause.

"See you in 30."

He logged off, and I giddily began my preparations…

––––––––––––

Eric knocked on my door. He was wearing his tennis cleats, his blue jeans, and no doubt some indie-rock T-shirt underneath that black hoodie of his. However, he didn't look intimidating at all; he was kind of adorable, in fact, in that wannabe-hipster kind of way. I let him in, and he toed off his sneakers like he always did. My luck: he was wearing ankle socks tonight, which was my favorite look (on him at least). I kindly offered him a beer. His reply?

"Whatever you're going to do, I think I'll need one." Oh, how correct he was…

I offered him a Corona. He eagerly sipped before plopping down on my futon. He swigged again, and then faced me, his short brown hair slightly messy as always.

"Alright," he started, "what's this endurance challenge you have in mind?"

"Simple, I tie you to this futon, and see what you can endure. 30 minutes is what I had in mind. Might be longer… if you're a wuss."

"I'm not a wuss!"

"Prove it to me."

Eric hesitated. "You didn't say anything about bondage."

"Trust me, it's light. Also, I'm still your friend first and foremost. Not going to do anything terrible to you… just having a bit of fun is all."

Eric hesitated again, but then chugged his beer once more, slammed it down on my end table, and resigned to his fate.

"Alright, what do I have to do?"

I grinned.

"OK, first, lay face down on this futon, your feet sticking out over the armrest."

Eric calmly did so, positioning his ankles right there on the armrest, his socked feet capable of full motion in the dull apartment air. I then pulled out my collection of zip ties. I slowly attached a zip to each of his ankles, and then used a separate set of zips to fasten his ankles to the futon armrest. Given that the armrest was slightly elevated above the seat of the futon mattress, Eric's feet were raised higher than the rest of his face-down body, which made my hooded friend look all the more deliciously helpless. I grabbed one last pair of zip ties that I had previously "looped" together, and simply pulled his arms behind his back and handcuffed them together with the zips. I stood back and admired Eric's predicament: this was a fantastic sight to see.

"You hate me?"

"Kinda," he said rather non-chalantly.

"Well, don't worry – it'll all be over soon… ish."

I pulled a chair over to the end of the futon. I brought over the small set of supplies I had assembled, and plopped down. There, in front of me, were two totally helpless socked Ericfeet: ankles bound to the armrest, toes pointed downward. I dragged a fingernail over his left sole – heel to toes – and watched as he choked on surprised laughter, his foot instinctively curling to try and protect itself. Gods, this was going to be fun…

I hooked the rim of Eric's right anklesock and SLOWLY dragged it over his heels, down his soles, and across those lovely,

lovely toes. I mainly wanted to make him feel helpless, but was also indulging my foot fetish to an almost unfathomable degree.

After all, a beautiful pair of Ericfeet were helpless in front of me, and I'll be damned if I wasn't going to play with them. Bound and barefoot, Eric was no doubt uneasy about what was going to happen next. I was now going to ease his nerves somewhat.

"OK, Eric, here's the game plan. I am going to time you for 30 minutes. During this time, I will relentlessly tickle these sexy bare feet of yours. Every few minutes, I am going to insert a $10 bill in-between your toes. Your job: to hold onto it with your toes. I am going to continue to tickle you while this goes on. If you drop a bill, then you lose it: plain and simple. If you hold onto it, then at the end of 30 minutes, you get to keep it. However, if you lose ALL the bills before the time is up, then you lose – and I begin to 'no-limit tickle' you for as long as I want. I didn't call it an endurance test for nothing."

There was a pause. I cheerfully inquired: "How does that sound?"

A pause. Then Eric spoke: "I really, really hate you."

I grinned. "I know – but look on the bright side: sooner we get started, the sooner it's over. So here we go!"

I already had a timer pre-set, and pressed START. It made an audible beep. I placed it on the floor next to Eric, sat back in my chair… and waited.

Eric's feet were tense. They were expecting the unrelenting torture of tickles… but all they felt was dry air. His toes nervously fidgeted, but all to no avail. I fucking loved watching them worry. This was heaven.

I then pulled out a giant, soft feather. I flicked his left heel with it. Pause. I flicked his right heel with it. Pause. The toes almost-clenched both times. I then began lightly scraping his right heel with the feather slowly, teasingly. I knew it only kinda tickled, and kept this up for a minute. Oh how those feet curled, showing me all ways the skin of his feet could expand and contract – what wonderful textures.

Then, without warning, I dropped the feather and did an all-out finger tickle assault on Eric's exposed soles, my fingernails wildly poking and scratching and scraping against Eric's too-ticklish feet.

He may have been holding it in before, but I was getting some deep, upper-register laughing from this boy, a kind I never heard before. It was obvious that he genuinely hated it – he tried getting out several protests before they were strangled by the next laugh wave – but that only encouraged me further. The best part was how with his hands tied behind his back while face-down, he couldn't move a lot, so while his body flailed around like a fish out of water, his bound feet never moved.

I then stopped and let him catch his breath. I took out my first $10 and folded it long ways, then folding it again so it was in quarters.

"Bill number one," I announced.

I eyed both of his delicious soles, and decided I'd make it easy on him: I slid it between the big and index toe of his left foot. Yet I didn't merely slide it in there: I slowly slid it in and out… and in… and out, over and over, tickling the space between his toes with soft money paper; I was rewarded with a fresh batch of reluctant giggles.

"Hold on!" I exclaimed, and suddenly Eric's foot clenched tightly, securing the note between his toes.

"You drop it you lose it," I reminded him.

"Dude, this is going to be really hard!"

"I said it was an endurance test: you can't be THAT surprised."

"Well, I know that, but HAHAHAHGAHHASTOP!!"

While he was talking, I went one toe over and inserted bill number two. A lot harder to squeeze it in what with the toes clenched but I did it. My favorite part about sliding in and out of clenched toes? Knowing they can't clench any further, which makes the tickling just that much sweeter…

There my victim was: one bound foot clenched with two bills in-between his toes, the other foot bare and nervous. I broke out my camera and snagged a picture: wanna save this sight for the memories.

My fingernails danced on the heel of the money foot, lightly, spider-like. The wispy gestures slowly made their way to his ticklish, ticklish soles, and I could hear him start to beg: "Please! Stop! I can't take this!" All of this fell on deaf ears.

I went one toe over and did more slide-tickling with yet another $10 bill. Eric was aggravated, ticklish, and helpless – I loved it.

Now, Eric's left foot had three bills wedged in, but his pinkie-toe slot was wide open. Instead of inserting a bill, though, I had a far more devious idea…

"Alright… time for test number one…"

"Oh god…" he groaned (and was correct to do so).

Even with his toes clenched, I managed to pull open the space of that pinkie-toe slot and inserted… a fuzzy little pipe cleaner…

Eric realized what it was. "DON'T YOU FUCKING DARE"

But it was too late. I began slowly dragging the pipe cleaner all along, tickling every nerve ending between those toes. Even though his body wanted to flail and get away, that foot had to remain clenched, lest it lose the cash. He had to force his foot to remain clenched – self-inflicted bondage as it were. I didn't even want to think of how badly his brain was short-circuiting.

Snapped another picture. 15 minutes left. Over the next 8, I inserted four bills into the other "toe slots", but by the second one Eric began yelling "GAH I FUCKING HAHAHATE YOU YOU HAHA SONOFAHAHABITCH!!", getting less coherent as time went on. Man I LOVED dragging money through his toes; so much that I then "readjusted" older slots just for fun.

I leaned back for a second: two bound, sweaty feet were in front of me, toes desperately clenching onto money.

"Alright, Eric. We got 6 minutes left. Let's savor them shall we?" All I got in reply was an inaudible groan from my barefoot victim.

It was at this point I broke out a big blue permanent marker, and began to draw a crude dollar sign on the sole of his left foot. Eric immediately yelped but then broke down into desperate laughter as I retraced that symbol again and again, the rest of his body flailing and flailing… but the toes were still clenched.

With minutes to go, I sat down on the floor in front of Eric's right foot and, starting with the heel at the top, began writing. "I," I repeated as I wrote, "Eric McCormack…"

"STOP!!" he yelled.

"Hereby declare that my feet…"

"NOOOOOHAHAOOO!!"

"Are the SOLE property of…"

"GAAAHHHH!!!"

And with that, the toes spastically unclenched, and all the money fell promptly to the ground. Eric officially lost. A pause. Then the timer beep. So close.

"Fuuuucccckkkk" was all I could hear drifting out of Eric's sweating, helpless body.

"Yes, fuck is correct good sir. I really do feel bad for you, but an agreement is an agreement, and I can't go back on an agreement."

Eric reluctantly sighed, "I know."

"Good. Now," I began, pushing my chair aside and kneeling so I was eye-level with his marker-stained soles, "we've firmly established that your feet are ticklish, but tell me: are they LICKLISH?"

"NOOOOOOOO!" he screamed, but it was already too late.

I dove in, smashing my face right into those soles and taking gigantic inhales of footsweat. My tongue then lashed out, eagerly lapping each foot in giant strokes, licking quickly and thoroughly. Remembering how much he hated being tickled between his toes, I made extra sure to have my tongue dart in and out of those between-toe spaces again and again and again. Eric weakly, vainly struggled, now wheezing out laughs when he was bellowing them before. My poor tickle slave was tired, but that was too damn bad 'cos I wasn't done with him yet…

An hour later, Eric's feet were glistening, positively coated with my saliva. I was satisfied. I broke out some scissors to cut his zip ties, and once his body was free, it instinctively curled up in the fetal position. Poor guy passed out mere moments later.

"Wake up," I said, lightly shoving Eric's body. His eyes groggily opened. "We're at your stop," I continued.

Eric noticed he was in the passenger seat of my car, and I had dropped him off at the front of his apartment. He noticed that his shoes were on, but…

"No socks?"

"Oh I'm keeping those. But, I think I made up for that with this."

I handed him a plain white envelope. He looked at me, and saw 8 sweat-stained $10 bills, and a single $100 bill.

"What's this for?" he asked.

"Dude, even though you lost, you fucking endured, man. You're still my friend, and I know submitting yourself to something like that took courage. Throw in my getting to keep your socks, and I call that money well earned…"

"You… you didn't have to do this…"

"And you didn't have to submit to my fetish fantasies… but you did."

"Well, thanks man."

"Thanks to you too. 'til next time, Eric…"

"Ditto."

With that, Eric got out of the car and I drove off. As Eric made it into his apartment, he went up to his bedroom and was ready to pass out for a whole week. He took off his shoes, but then noticed something was written on his feet with red marker: NOW IMAGINE WHAT YOU'D HAVE TO DO FOR $200…

Two weeks later, he called to inquire about what that would entail…

CHAPTER FIVE

HAPPY

"Drunk girls know that love is an astronaut: it comes back but it's never the same." – James Murphy

"Why aren't you smiling, David?"

The camera adjusted, gaining focus. Slowly David's face came into view: lean and muscular, a thin layer of fuzz covering his chin and neck from days of not having shaved. It was an almost-beard. Dark-haired and sullen-eyed, David was staring at the monitor in front of him. The computerized voice repeated:

"David, why aren't you smiling?"

David let out a dejected sigh: "'cos I'm not happy, CAIRO. I thought that even you could figure that out." David hesitated for a moment, and then stood up to walk down the corridors. CAIRO adjusted its camera yet again to get a glimpse of its subject walking away. CAIRO had no emotion, but could sense that the health of its subject was in question.

David went back to his sleeping quarters. He saw the date and grimaced a little. David has been on NASA's first moon base for well over 17 months now, which was a record by itself, but made even more impressive by the fact that he was the youngest astronaut (28) to ever go on a mission of this magnitude. This was to be his last month on the base, but got word just two days ago that his mission had been extended by a whole month. He was stuck here on this station with CAIRO – the automated astronaut-maintenance system – as his only company. CAIRO resembled HAL 9000 a little too close for David's comfort, but what else could he do? CAIRO still made him macaroni and cheese for dinner, gauged his heart rate while jogging on the treadmill, and warned him of debris storms when he was outside, doing maintenance or conducting experiments. CAIRO was an immaculately well-constructed mechanical system, and its purpose was to make any and all astronauts in its care as lively and at-ease as possible. All these months later, David was coming around to liking the damn thing, but upon hearing news of his extension, talking to an emotion-free series of circuits like CAIRO was the last thing he needed right now.

Back in his quarters, David – dressed in a loose white maintenance suit but without shoes or socks – tapped on the video screen right above his bed. He loaded up his log of the last few video transmissions he received from back on Earth – these were the things that he treasured the most during his time on the station. Three of them were from Aly, his fiancée. Aly was a sweet young red-headed girl who thought the world of David. She was into scrapbooking and was looking to start up her own arts and crafts store – easy to do when sharing in on the salary of an astronaut. Since they could only transmit or receive one video at a time, each entry was like its own video blog, and Aly would update him on what she was doing this week, any newspaper articles that mentioned his name, and – of course – how much she (and her three cats) missed him. Each entry was sweet, yet repetitive. Being on a moon base for a year and a half had given David a lot of time to think about their relationship. Watching these videos always reminded him of why he fell for her in the first place, yet since arriving at the station, David's thoughts began thinking of someone else…

The night before he left before his weeklong detox and prep at the NASA center, David was out having drinks with his friend Brian. Although many friends were out with them, they all petered out pretty early, and soon Brian and David were alone, drunk off of a ton of Blue Moons (they lost count of how many they had, but were confident they had breached the double-digits). Brian was 26, blond, handsome, and had a great career at a large PR firm. He had a special bond with David, as the two could talk about just about anything to each other: their embarrassing moments, their secret desires, everything. Now, drunk at a downtown bar on a Tuesday night with virtually no one else around, Brian and David were getting in a bit of sentimental mood: they were really going to miss each other. Brian was finishing up some thoughts:

"Oh, and before I forget," he said before slamming his beer on the table with a bit of clumsy force, "I really wanted to wish you and Aly a really good time."

"What good time? I'm only going to be video-messaging her for 18 months. That's about as long as a long-distance relationship gets!"

"Well, you know what I mean. Seriously: she's a lucky lady."

David paused for a second and stared at Brian. "What do you mean 'she's a lucky lady'? You make it sound like you've been pining for her yourself…"

"Well, I have been pining for someone, David."

"Who?"

The air was thick with silence. Brian simply stared back, obviously emboldened by the drink, and looked at his long friend with a warm smile: "… you."

David stared at his younger friend with intent: was he serious? Was this some elaborate going away gag or something? But no. It was clear that Brian was really, truly pining for his good friend David, and the vulnerability shone through his eyes: that confession really took it out of him, and his fate now lived and died by David's words.

"Well," started David, "this is… unexpected to say the least."

"Pfft, tell me about it." Brian seemed to be very non-chalant about David's reaction. "You don't know how hard it is to secretly want to be around your smart, funny, and sexy friend all the time…"

"Sexy?"

"David," started Brian, "I'd worship your body 100 times over if you'd let me."

David's brain, a bit hazy from booze, was processing all of this – and was unsure of what to feel. At first, yes, being the object of desire of one of your good friends for years on end was a bit much to take in. However, "sexy"? No one had ever called him sexy. In college, girls called him hot, and Aly never went beyond calling his body "nice", but "sexy"? Being called that – with genuine sincerity – made David feel really, really good. He kind of liked the idea of being an idealized sexual object, lusted upon from afar. David wasn't an egoist; he just found such a compliment very flattering and… kind of hot. His brain was instantly making all sorts of connections, and thought about Brian – and how kind he was… and how nice he looked … and – wait, how nice he looked?

"When you say worship," David started without thinking, "what do you mean?"

A spark went off in Brian's eyes.

"I mean ... well, have you ever had anything besides your cock sucked on?"

David thought for a second. "No."

"Well come here," started Brian, motioning for David to lean in.

Brian's mouth was at David's neck, and he could feel Brian's warm breath bouncing off of his skin. A light kiss was planted – intimate but not romantic nor sexual. Just... nice. Suddenly Brian's hands began moving slowly up David's arms and into his armpits – David giggled just a bit, and laughed. This kind of playful prodding – was nice. It was fun. It was... turning him on a bit. Then the fingers began slowly tracing down David's ribs as the warm breathing continued on his neck. Then the fingers went for the kill and squeezed David's thigh. David jumped and squeaked a bit, but upon smiling, said, "Go on."

The fingers felt down the seams of David's jeans, and eventually pulled up David's ankle into Brian's lap. The fingers circled the outside of David's tennis shoes with a playful kind of stroking, up and down like the feet themselves were sexual objects. The fingers then began untying the laces and slowly slipped the shoe off. Weirdly enough, David was totally digging this. Not that the sex he had with Aly or any other girl in college wasn't fun, but fetish play was suddenly opening up whole new doors to him. The shoe came off, and then the fingers worked their way up the socks. David was uncontrollably smiling with pleasure once again. This was actually REALLY fun. Feeling Brian's fingers run across the soles of his socks, lightly scratching the bare, ticklish feet contained within – it was too much. Then the sock got ripped off, and – all underneath the table of this dinky little bar – David was receiving his first real foot massage of his life. Perhaps it was the booze or perhaps it was the stress of leaving for a year and a half, but fuck if this didn't feel like bliss. It was like the best kind of foreplay he had ever experienced. Occasionally the nails would tickle the soles, but for the most part the skin-on-skin rubbing contact was sending the drunken astronaut into the stratosphere of sheer ecstasy. Of course, they couldn't go any further without being detected by the bar staff, but after about ten minutes of non-stop drunken fun, Brian handed David back his sock and leaned over to say "You think you enjoyed that? That was just the beginning my friend." Brian left a quick kiss on the nape of David's neck and whispered "We'll talk more when you get back. You will be missed." Brian then departed and David was left alone in this bar, drunk off his ass, his right foot bared, and his mind flooded with a ton of thoughts that were totally new and totally alien to him.

The next week of detox and last-minute training occupied virtually all of his time, but the thought of Brian and fondling and playing like that – they were on the backburner of his mind. They echoed in his late night thoughts on the space station and in his dreams sometimes. Now, he was looking to see which one of Brian's messages was in the video queue. David loaded it up as he usually does, and watched the whole thing. Of course, since every incoming and outgoing call was screened by NASA (and CAIRO for that matter), Brian's update was basic: he talked about some big clients he was working for, shared some good celebrity run-in stories, and mentioned what David's other friends were up to (Heather had a baby!). Yet it was that goodbye with the wink at the end that kept David wondering. His updates from Brian were every two months or so (which was unlike Aly, who sent a new video every week), but strangely, David watched the Brian videos more. Even though at this moment they were not helping his state of mind (staying another month meant that he couldn't see Brian for another month as well), it brought him a little assurance: there were people from all sides awaiting his return, with a mixture of warmth and lust, envy and delight. If it weren't for those feelings, David thought he would go insane out here in the dark nothingness.

Yet this warmth was temporary. David put on his sneakers without socks and went to the small gym area. One of CAIRO's robotic arms greeted him with a towel, which he then wrapped around the top of his treadmill. He just began running like hell, exhausting his body so that his mind couldn't stray too far, the TV ahead playing the latest crappy sitcoms that he liked so much (NASA could beam them up to him, but it took well over a week for him to get anything new). As sweat started pouring down his face, the physical anguish soon triggered his emotional pain, and soon violent tears were mixing in with his sweat, one indistinguishable from the other. His mind began thinking in pointed sentences: "How DARE they keep me here another goddamn month! Away from my family! Away from my friends! And, worst of all, away from Brian!" He thought about that wink from Brian at the end of that last transmission, and that did it. David screamed as loud as he possibly could in an unbridled fury, and then walked right off of the treadmill, lying down on the floor in anguish, as unhappy as he's ever been.

Tears were still going, as one of CAIRO's mobile cameras managed to extend down to right where David was laying. All David could see was a giant, unemotional camera eye staring back at him. He really didn't want to deal with a robot right now, but he didn't really have much of a choice.

"What's wrong, David?" it asked in its measured, warm tone.

"What the fuck do you think is wrong?"

"You don't appear to be your regular self today."

"WELL OF COURSE NOT!" he yelled. "Can your fuckin' motherboard even process emotion? Even a fuckin' ounce of it? I'm pretty damn upset right now. I feel... alone."

"But I'm here, David."

"Yeah, but you can't make me happy."

There was a bit of a pause as CAIRO processed its thoughts.

"I can try."

David, frustrated, stood up and looked right into the robotic arm camera that was hovering over him. "You can try to make me happy? Do you even know what happiness is to a guy like me?"

CAIRO was curious. "What physical attributes do you exhibit while being happy?"

David snorted a bit. The dumb robot didn't even fuckin' know.

"I'd be smiling, CAIRO. I'd be grinning from ear to ear so much that I couldn't even think about anything else. That's when I'm happy. I'd fuckin' love to see you try."

"But David, my main mission is to make sure your health and functions are sustainable for service."

David took off his sweaty sneakers and began to make his way back to his quarters. Soon tossing off one last, fatal remark: "Well you got a new mission now, CAIRO. Your goal is to try and make me the happiest goddamn person in the world. I really can't wait to see what the fuck you come up with." Dave's bare skin across the floor echoed in the white, perpetually-clean hallway. The camera gained focus on its subject as he turned the corner into his room. Quietly, its processors began churning away – it had a new task at hand.

The "night lights" went on, simulating some vague sense of late evening so that David could maintain something closely resembling a sleep schedule. There were now just a small, faint florescent over his bed that David could turn off at will. Here he was, re-reading James Joyce's *Ulysses* for the umpteenth time, feeling painfully, terribly alone. He shut the lights off and curled up in his bed, facing the spotless wall right next to it. Wrapped in his blanket, he felt somewhat comforted – but not a whole lot.

After napping for a few hours, he woke up to see – his room in the evening light setting. This was odd. He didn't normally get up before CAIRO reset the lights to daytime. He looked at the time on a nearby monitor – yes, it was 10AM, definitely when sunlight should be out. "CAIRO?" he shouted. David waited. Nothing. Something was definitely wrong now. David walked out into the main hallway – still barefoot, wearing just his space jumper – and noticed everything was in night mode – only a faint row of lights overhead illuminated his pathway. He kept on walking until he saw that a light was on in the Isolation Room. That was even stranger – the Isolation Room only had drop-down monitors for emergencies, but for the most part was simply used when an astronaut needed to concentrate on something and needed no distractions to speak of. To have that room and only that room have its lights on, as if someone was in there – was actually a bit terrifying.

David slowly creaked the door open, and saw that there was a chair simply sitting in the middle of the room, facing the door. David looked around – and saw nothing. He slowly walked in, one cautious step after another.

"Hello there, David. Why don't you take a seat?"

David looked around – wasn't this supposed to be the Isolation Room? Did CAIRO really have access here as well? David looked around, and could see a camera arm in the corner – apparently the corners of the wall were removable, which means that CAIRO pretty much had free reign. This was... unsettling.

"CAIRO, what's going on?"

"Have a seat, David. I'll soon tell you everything you need to know."

David sat down cautiously. His toes kind of felt around the floor a bit, exhibiting his nervousness and anxiety.

"Alright, CAIRO: what the hell is this about?"

"David, last night you tasked me with a very important charge: to make you happy. When you are happy, this usually physically manifests itself in the form of a smile. Can we agree upon these simple principles?"

Dave was a bit flustered. "Um... I guess."

"Good. Now David..."

"Ya know you can just call me Dave. It's OK, CAIRO. It's not like you've been saying 'David' for a year-and-a-fuckin'-half."

"Noted. Now Dave, what would you say makes you happy?"

"Going home would make happy right now."

"That is something that will make you happy in the short-term, but I'm wondering about something that makes you happy in general."

"Well fuck, I don't know. A cold beer. A beautiful day in the spring. Taking off your work socks after a long 12-hour shift. A sweaty, efficient evening of fucking. I don't know CAIRO. Probably best would be..." David realized he was dipping a bit into sentimentality – possibly even schmaltz – but didn't care, "to simply be in an evening where you're in the arms of someone you love dearly."

"And who would that be, Dave?"

"Aly, naturally."

The response was instantaneous: "Not Brian?"

A flint of anger surged through David's body. "... What?"

"Well Dave," CAIRO started, "I've been watching your habits in the past while. You mention Aly as being important in your life, yet you've watched the transmissions from Brian more times than all of the transmissions from Aly together. You seem to like replaying that moment when he winks at you over and over again"

"OK, I've had enough of this shit, CAIRO!"

Suddenly, the automated door for the Isolation Room closed and locked in front of David.

"Dave, we need to get this taken care of. My goal is to make you happy before you even leave this room – and presently, I feel that all I've done is upset you. We'll find what makes you tick before too long."

David stood up in a rage. "CAIRO, now is not the time to fuck around with me! Let me go!"

The faint hum of mechanics was all that filled the pregnant pause between the two sentient beings.

"OK, Dave, but I'm still doing the weekly infection sweep of the halls. I'm going to need to sanitize you before you go back out there. I'm sorry for not tending to you before."

David cocked an eyebrow, knowing that such a thing was very unlike CAIRO's usually-organized, to-the-point behavior – but who was he to question? David raised his hands in the air, and just like every time that had happened prior, two sleek robotic arms extended down from the ceiling (so there was some stuff up there!), the rounded fingertips moving in closer to David's hips so that it could start removing the jumpsuit. Without even thinking, though, David – somewhat already untrusting of CAIRO, backed to his left side somewhat subconsciously as the arms went to remove the jumpsuit. He accidentally ran into the soft, rounded robotic fingers which were kneading into David's sides, and he laughed a bit. "Hey, watch it!"

The camera zoomed in.

"Dave… were you smiling?"

"Um, yeah, sorry. The fingers just tickled me a bit."

"Tick-le?"

"Yeah," David replied, non-chalantly.

There was silence. Suddenly the robotic fingers begin tickling the air in front of them, slowly moving towards David, menacingly.

"Tick-le," the voice coldly repeated.

"Wha… ?"

David instinctively backed up, but the arms descended far too quickly, and soon were placed perfectly in his sides. The fingers began to oscillate, and boy did those perfectly smoothed and rounded robofingers tickle! David's mouth stretched into a grotesque distortion of its former self, as a laugh simply tore its way out of his body. It was violent, sudden, and unexpected. David's eyes shot open wide in surprise.

"WHAT THE FUCK, CAI…"

He didn't even had time to finish the sentence: the robofingers managed to sneak their way right up into David's armpits, kneading the soft patch of flesh right next to the top parts of his ribcage, just tapping it repeatedly like a telegraph – awaiting a response from the tickles on the other end. David drew his arms in as close as he could to escape the torment, but the arms were deep in there, and there wasn't a moment when they weren't moving, twisting David's armpit hairs slowly, pinching and poking and tormenting his flesh without stopping for a second.

David fell on the floor but the arms continued to tickle and tickle and tickle. His bare heels began grinding into the floor and pushing his way back into the wall, but the arms remained there, like they were glued to his sensitive areas, just tickling and teasing more and more. David was choking on his uncontrollable laughter. As his eyes clenched shut and the smiles tumbled out, David failed to see a second pair of robotic arms had come down from the ceiling and proceeded to grab his ankles, turning his body around in the process. David looked up and yelled profanities, but as he did so, the finger in his pits suddenly pulled out and wrapped their way around his wrists, soon lifting his whole body up off the ground.

"Oh no you fuckin' don't!"

David struggled as much as his strength would allow, but before long, his arms and legs were stretched out like a piñata, belly to the floor, his whole body stretched and suspended about ten feet in the air. His hands were held in front of him, his legs held behind him, his body sagging helplessly in between. David fought as much as he perceptibly could, but it was obvious that CAIRO's grip on him was way too tight – he was his caretaker's own fuckin' puppet, and the show was just getting started.

A camera attached to a robotic arm careened down and stared at David in the face. CAIRO's unemotional voice spoke as if nothing was happening.

"Are you ready, Dave?"

"Hey fucktard! Do you see what kind of position I'm in?"

"Yes – I am the one putting you in it."

"That's not what I meant, jag-off! What the literal fuck are you doing?"

"Dave, I'm making you happy."

"By what, tickling me? You're not making me happy – you're pissing me off!"

"I disagree, Dave. You said that you were happy when you were smiling. And by performing tick-le on you, your smile grows wider than anything I have seen in my video archive. I think tick-le is quite effective."

"That's not how it works, CAIRO."

"I have concluded that the wider the smile gets, and the higher the pitch of your voice goes, the happier you are. All I'm trying to do is to make you happy."

"CAIRO, I…"

Two additional cybernetic arms – which had emerged with no warning – suddenly jabbed fingers into David's ribcage, and they fuckin' tickled.

"Gah-ha-had stop it! Pl-e-e-ase!"

"I have to override your request Dave. You obviously struggle against tick-le, so I have to force you to receive it, much how I'm programmed to make sure you reach your daily amount of nutritional supplements. It's for your own good."

David tried to formulate a response, but it was drowned out in the stunted, sputtering laughter that he was spewing forth.

The round robotic fingers were having quite a bit of fun dancing in David's ribs, moving a bit closer to the nipples and then gradually making their way back to his spine, still tickling the whole time, kneading his flesh, playfully poking the spaces in between his ribs. However CAIRO was figuring out ways to tickle, it was working damn well.

Slowly, fingers teased the area right underneath David's ribcage, playfully poking and scratching the front of David's tummy, curious as to what kind of reaction it would produce. When something caused David's synapses to fire off the scale, like when CAIRO found that by doing the "pinching" motion of tickling across his belly his voice shot up two octaves, CAIRO learned the technique and began finding variations on it. CAIRO was learning that one particular "style" of tickling didn't work when prolonged: it had to switch things up, trying unexpected angles at off-beat times, constantly moving and changing so that the laughter pouring out of David's mouth was constant – and entirely against his will.

David's lungs began heaving and panting perceptibly. CAIRO was monitoring his heart rate and health, and decided to give him a break. As David caught more bucket breaths to try and regain at least some of his strength, CAIRO had one of those smoothed robofingers trace along David's spine, scratching rather softly at different points just to test reactions. Sometimes it'd tease a muscle on his back, other times glide along the curve of his neck, occasionally circling around to his armpits just because it would definitely produce a laugh – his armpits always did. The arms then moved around to David's securely bound feet – those toes had been flexing and wiggling the whole time. David felt like passing out, and then he felt it: that small, barely noticeable scratching along his heel. It was on both feet, and it almost felt like a hummingbird wing was continually flapping against his the thickest part of his heel. It tickled a bit, sure – but it wasn't stopping. Those fingers were barely scratching his heels, but they weren't stopping, like pair of tickle-crazed insects were just feeding off of those heels alone. Sure, his feet tried moving sideways and flexed and curled, but the goddamn tickling wasn't stopping.

David's hesitant giggles were starting to choke out as full-blown laughs. The grimace on his face was intense: he was doing everything he could to fight it, but CAIRO was pushing buttons he didn't even know he had. That perpetual, constant, unstoppable feathering of his heel was driving him up the wall. His bare feet were practically having seizures of agony, doing every miniscule thing they could to fight the overwhelming power of tickle that was assaulting them – but all these efforts were in vain. David had limits, barriers, and exhaustion walls that he was hitting. CAIRO didn't have any of these.

Once the heel feathering started getting David's vocal chords regurgitating laughs in the most painful of ways, those tickling fingers began moving toeward. They started scratching right in that sweet spot where heel and sole meet and it felt like David was being teased in a place he had never even been touched before. Scratchy, scratchy, scratchy. It didn't stop. Although the toes flexed and screamed to try and get away, it was obvious their fates were sealed. The fingers kept moving up, scratching those too-sensitive soles, and it was like they were having a field day. Once again, David's voice shot up an octave, his laughing became even more pathetic than before. David was practically pleading with CAIRO now, but certainly not in any language resembling English. The robofingers scratched upward slowly, slowly, soon attacking the balls of David's feet and then the base of the toes, alternating between scratching them and then simply poking David's foot right in the center and then wiggling that finger around. The corners of his mouth almost hurting from the ridiculous strain they were being put through. CAIRO, meanwhile, was simply watching. Observing. And worst of all, it was learning.

The more the toes splayed and tried to escape their inevitable fate, the more CAIRO learned what tickle techniques were working best. The scratching worked great, especially when followed by a nice stroking. Done with David's helpless feet, the fingers began to lightly pinch his flesh through his jumpsuit around his ankles, and then up the calves, and then lightly fingering the back of his knees. Once it discovered that the back of his knees were producing whole chokes of laughter, the arms that were restraining his legs pulled his body taught – there was now no way those knees would be able to bend even a fraction of an inch to escape their tickle torture. David's mind, so far gone already, was snapping now – his body had already enjoyed the spasms his nerves put him through, largely because it gave him a brief, fleeting moment of release, but CAIRO was preventing him from even enjoying that.

The robofingers almost bounced in that soft spot on the back of his knees, poking that sensitive, fleshy patch before scratching a bit on the outside. David's laughs mutated into whines during this, as CAIRO's devious itches proved to be the thing that worked him into overdrive. Then, without pause, the hands began pinching David's inner thighs, and his voice reached full on soprano heights. "FUCCCCCK!" he cried out, before drowning in a sea of laughter. CAIRO took this in. The pinching slowly went up his thighs, closer and closer to his hanging balls, and David's last bit of fight emerged, trying to prevent the robot from toying with his junk.

Yet it was all in vain. Soon, the robotic arms were reaching around and merely poking around his pelvis: slightly below the belly button, an inch away from his balls on his thighs, square on each side of his hips, merely teasing the area around his genitals. David was sweating.

A flash of lasers suddenly appeared and disappeared, and David wondered if any hit him. Then, he found out that they did: in an instant, his jumpsuit fell off his body in tatters. Being how he was belly-parallel with the floor, the roboarms restraining his arms and legs proceeded to lightly tip him upwards, and the pieces that remained on his back simply slid off his bum onto the floor. He was still suspended in air, but practically in a standing position now, feet nearly parallel with the floor. He was fucked.

He would've screamed at the robot. He would've asked how the hell nudity was going to help this "experiment", but the connection between his conscious thoughts and his mouth was severed long ago. David merely panted. That was pretty much all he could do now: pant and laugh for his new robot master.

Another robotic arm had extended down from the ceiling – David didn't even want to look so looked down at himself and – he was half-erect. He almost didn't even notice it – that poking around his crotch was enough to tease him to half-mast. Fuck. Even as he stared at his junk in amazement, the new arm slowly craned into view: it was the brush-scrubbing arm from the shower. With small, wispy bristles along its rounded head, it sometimes could whirl around at high speeds – which now made David absolutely terrified about the fact that it was positioning itself right underneath his balls.

He weakly struggled in his bonds, but he knew better than CAIRO did that it was useless. The little wispy bristles made contact with the undersides of his testicles, and he nearly wanted to jump out of his skin. Fuck was he sensitive and fuck were those sagging sacks of sensitivity not ready for such a goddamn sensation. CAIRO's arm merely moved around a bit, lightly teasing his flesh, and David wanted to cry – it tickled SO MUCH! Little, devious lightning flecks murdering his synapses with each passing nano-second. David was laughing so hard, which, in many ways, was his reality right now: he lived in a realm of ticklish laughter – and that is all that he knew.

Then, David heard that whirring mechanical sound that he had so gotten used to over the past year and a half: the scrubber's head was beginning to rotate… slowly. Gradually, those soft little bristles began to circle David's most sensitive of areas, and his body began to spasm violently. A whole new world of tickle suddenly shot open. The whirling brush was only so lightly touching the back of David's balls, but, then, gradually began to rotate, going from the back of his balls to the bottom of them, slowly working their way to the front, attacking his glands like they were marked by an assassin. Full-blown tears were now streaming from David's eyes and all of this tickling of his privates was causing his erection to get just a little bit more engorged than before.

This wasn't news to CAIRO, however, which had been watching David the entire time he's been here – which meant that, of course, it even observed him masturbating. CAIRO had determined that humans like having their genitals played with in a pleasurable way, although each was different in its approach. David never liked to leave a huge cumshot for whatever reason, and instead just wound up teasing himself to the edge before backing off, time and time again. However, merely repeating the exact same thing wasn't going to work for CAIRO. Given that David's smile had already mutated several times since this "session" began, CAIRO was certain that an orgasm was the only way to get David's smile as wide as it could possibly be.

The whirling brush was slowing to a stop. As it did so, it removed itself entirely from David's balls. Panting, sweating, and trying not to cry from this merciless tickle abuse, David imagined in his mind a place that wasn't in this room, much less on this orbiting satellite rock. He envisioned himself laying safely in his bed at home, the morning sun peaking in through the window to wake him up, hearing a softly whispered "good morning" come from the other side of the bed, turning his own body around to see Brian's sweet face looking back at…

Wait, Brian? What the hell did Brian have to do with this? Could it…

"OK, Dave – I have a surprise for you."

CAIRO's intonation was as far from sympathetic as you could possibly imagine.

"CAIRO," whispered David, weakly, "Please, let me go. My voice is hoarse, and I don't know if I can…"

David heard the sound of another compartment opening from overhead, and down came another arm, but, wait, this was a tube. A blue tube that – oh no, it couldn't be.

"CAIRO… is that the…"

"Yes, Dave: it is liquid transportation cable used on this station base."

David's eyes opened as widely as they could – he was looking terror in the eyes.

After all, David knew exactly what that cable could do. It was like a space hose: if CAIRO had to transfer a part of the water supply from one part of the base to another, remote part of the base, it couldn't simply carry a bucket. Instead, this special tube was used as a direct link from one water supply to another. Of course, hooking up a hose by itself wasn't going to do the job (the gravity was too low for that), so scientists developed this special cable wherein a small electrical impulse could cause the cable to pulse in one direction or another. Instead of the water merely floating in the air, it would be "squeezed along" the tube because the tube itself was pulsating towards one direction. It was a very cost-effective breakthrough that no doubt had made millions of dollars for the inventor that came up with it. For David, however, it was a whole new nightmare.

"CAIRO, I BEG OF YOU PLEASE DON'T DO THIS!"

"It's for your own good, Dave. You wanted to be happy, right?"

And with that, the mouth of this blue hose began to swallow the head of David's penis, soon encompassing the rim, then the shaft, and somehow working its way straight down to the base. There was Dave: suspended in the air by four robotic arms, completely naked, and with a giant blue hose attached to his dick. Humiliation didn't even begin to describe it...

David's eyes cringed as much as they could: he was simply waiting for that first, dreaded pulse. He waited... and waited... and... well, maybe it wasn't going to...

SUCK. The first pulse was incredible. The interior of this space hose was remarkably soft, and to suddenly feel it gently grab a hold the base of his cock and suddenly work it was up the shaft, past the rim of the head and finally give the head a bit of a squeeze itself – well, it felt incredible. David wouldn't admit it to anyone ever, but...

SUCK. There it went again. It wasn't as much pleasurable, though, as it was completely overwhelming. Sure, it felt good, but David didn't really have a say, the machine merely SUCKed when it wanted to, which already SUCK holy crap it was increasing. It seemed that each time it did it; David's train of thought was SUCK goddammit, CAIRO!

David seriously tried to struggle but that vile space hose was latched on firmly to his manhood, and it was thoroughly enjoying torturing him. The frequency of the pulses was increasing ever so slowly, and David began to make all sorts of moans to accompany each one. He wasn't proud of it, but the feeling of the soft hose against his penis was proving to be too much – it was, in a sense, winning the battle of his senses, and there was almost nothing he could do.

David's face twisted into a grimace, now trying his best to fight off the machine. It doesn't matter how good it felt – he just didn't want a space hose to determine when he had an orgasm. Each SUCK that happened made David's thoughts of "fight this monstrosity!" get a little quieter each time. He eventually just abandoned the whole thing, because devil be damned, this felt amazing. Having some outside force control his cock was a bit terrifying, but also turning out to be a bit exciting, because he truly didn't know what was going to happen next. His body was drained of all of its energy, so to have one single (diabolical) pump bring him closer and closer to the orgasm of his life – well, it was more than worth it.

The pumps were getting more rapid, and CAIRO could see that David's heart rate was increasing: a climax was just around the corner. The big dumb smile of his was certainly widening the closer he got, though. Seeing this as an opportunity, the robofingers placed themselves right outside of David's armpits, and right as his voice starting getting into that high-pitched "I'm gonna cum!" threshold, the fingers dived right into those flesh patches, lightly teasing his ticklish armpits just as his cock was tingling with excitement and oozing precum. Not expecting the sharp sensation, David's body jolted a bit, and that's all that needed to happen: David shot a monstrous, threatening load of cum. His entire cock quaked with gooey spasms of joy, his body flexing as much as it could while restrained, and each pump feeling like it was draining gallons of energy out of the boy. The cock shots were getting smaller as they went, but boy were there a ton of them. David, now with his mind completely empty of thought, tilted his head back and pleasantly sighed. He had never felt this good in his life.

A good 15 minutes had passed, and nothing happened. David was just blissfully alone his thoughts, his balls completely drained, and his body barely able to move an inch. When his groggy head did try to readjust itself, the ever-present CAIRO camera eye made its way down to make eye-contact with the boy.

"How do you feel, Dave?"

"I… I hate… you."

"But Dave, I was only helping. Your smile was wider than I have ever seen it. It appears that you were truly happy."

"CAIRO, just let me go."

"But why Dave?"

"'cos… well c'mon, 'cos you're done with your… fun."

"Dave, I thought you wanted to be constantly happy."

"CAIRO, there is only one way that I could be truly happy, and that's if…"

"I think I understand, Dave."

"… Understand what?"

"You want to see him."

"Who?"

"Brian."

"No, CAIRO, what I meant was…"

"It will take some time to get him here, Dave. Placing a decoy file with Brian's information into NASA's database takes time, but I should be able to do it. There is a flight already scheduled to bring in your replacement in a month's time."

"CAIRO, that's not what I…"

"If that is what will truly make you happy, Dave, I will make sure it gets done. It is, after all, my new priority to make you happy."

"CAIRO! LISTEN TO ME!"

"Now, according to my instruments, your skin has become rather sensitive following orgasm. Do you think a tick-le would work well on you now?"

"CAIRO PLEASE I BEG OF YOU TO…"

David still tried to fight, even though he was still hopelessly bound. The first robofinger traced a line up his sole, and David found out that in space, no one could hear you scream.

CHAPTER SIX

THE CHAT

Strangely, some of my best writing I think has come from IM conversations I've had. When I met my boyfriend, I tended to send entire stories-worth of horny missives to him through a small little chat window, and was sometimes amazed by how detailed they were for being "in the moment" (he, bless his heart, has saved each and every one). Personally, though, I never saved anything, largely 'cos I never thought they'd make great material, which said boyfriend has contested with. So when a random (and quite nice) guy IM'd me online, I decided it'd be fun to save the finished work, and, as you'll see, I'm damn glad I did...

VICTIM: so if you could tickle torture me as much and as long as you wanted

VICTIM: in detail, how would you do it?

VICTIM: and there's no taboo

VICTIM: you can tickle me anywhere

TICKLER: Well, in short, I'd have you tied spread-eagle to my bed, but you'd be fully clothed

TICKLER: And blindfolded.

TICKLER: Maybe a Tickle or "Lick Track" playing in your ears

TICKLER: 'cos if there's anything a good 'ler knows, it's that it's all in the build up

TICKLER: Tickling a foot is one thing

VICTIM: *smiles* that's right

TICKLER: But to have the fingers tapping on the soles of your sneakers, toyingly…

VICTIM: there's prep involved

TICKLER:… that's devious

VICTIM: like my stroking and teasing

TICKLER: To have those fingers stroke and trace the insteps of those sneakers

TICKLER: To tap along the button of your jeans

TICKLER: To glide across the fabric of your T-shirt

TICKLER: THAT is where the tension builds.

TICKLER: Feet are especially fun

TICKLER: 'cos after all the tapping is done, the sneaker slowly comes off

TICKLER: And then your socked foot involuntarily wiggles at its new freedom

TICKLER: It's even worse knowing that your 'ler is a master foot fetishist

TICKLER: 'cos you know he savors every goddamn second and every single moment.

TICKLER: He WANTS them to wiggle

VICTIM: *shivers* indeed

TICKLER: You FEEL his nose press up right between your socked big and first toe

TICKLER: The slight scraping of the fingers at your heels

TICKLER: Circling

TICKLER: Teasing

TICKLER: Never fully tickling

TICKLER: Hinting, always

TICKLER: Then it's two socked feet

TICKLER: The finger tracing and circling around the elastic rims of those socks

TICKLER: Playing with its food.

TICKLER: All of this just to make you feel more helpless

TICKLER: 'cos you want to be barefoot and over with

TICKLER: Instead: you're an h'orderves

TICKLER: Your master is savoring those details

TICKLER: Each smell

TICKLER: Each hair on your toe

TICKLER: It wants to envelop those toes like a moist sock

TICKLER: It's hungry for them

TICKLER: And yet its patient

TICKLER: And then the tickling starts

TICKLER: Those nails scraping along the sock fabric

TICKLER: Sometimes scratching your arches

TICKLER: Sometimes not

TICKLER: Playing with the sides of your feet

TICKLER: Poking the places in-between toes

TICKLER: Proving that the tops of your feet really are ticklish and loving it

TICKLER: But then those spidery fingers move up your legs

TICKLER: Your shins

TICKLER: The too-ticklish backs of your knees

VICTIM: yessss

VICTIM: very ticklish there haha

TICKLER: You're fucking horny and your master knows it, but even as he taps your hips, drilling index fingers right into them, your crotch remains untouched

TICKLER: Much like the socks, those fingers circle the rims of your boxers... but nothing yet

TICKLER: The fingering of nipples through shirt fabric

TICKLER: It hurts but it hurts so good

VICTIM: *shivers*

TICKLER: Then, those fingers camp out around those armpits

TICKLER: You try and flex to close those gaps – but you're tied too tight

TICKLER: Your open, airy armpits have never felt so exposed.

TICKLER: Those hands aren't at the armpits, they're right outside them

TICKLER: The fingertips right at the top of the rib on each side

TICKLER: And they tap.

TICKLER: index middle ring pinky

TICKLER: Tapping in a row

TICKLER: Then pausing

TICKLER: Tapping

TICKLER: Pausing

TICKLER: Sometimes they scratch a bit

TICKLER: And you are trying so fucking hard not to giggle

TICKLER: But you can't.

TICKLER: They squeak out

TICKLER: They are more powerful than you

TICKLER: Then the index fingers start crawling into those armpit tickle holes

TICKLER: Dragging closer

TICKLER: Tickling the flesh through the shirt fabric

TICKLER: Trying to twist the ticklish armpit hairs around.

VICTIM: duuuuuuuuuuuuuuuuuuuuuuuuude

TICKLER: Teasingly tickling

TICKLER: Ticklingly teasingly

TICKLER: It is devious

TICKLER: It tickles but worse than that, it almost tickles

TICKLER: Fuck those almost-tickles – they're even worse, 'cos they're not quite there but fuck do they tickle.

TICKLER: And then I get up

TICKLER: And your hardwired body is awake and… wondering what will happen next.

TICKLER: nothing.

TICKLER: Silence.

TICKLER: Then you hear it

TICKLER: *snip snip*

TICKLER: Scissors.

TICKLER: Just snipping in the air.

TICKLER: Then a hand grabs your pant leg

TICKLER: And starts working its way up

TICKLER: The scissors are hungry for boyfabric

TICKLER: And they are devouring the sides of your pants

TICKLER: Shins, knees, all the way to the belt loop

TICKLER: And suddenly, your only pair of pants is ruined

TICKLER: But they haven't got to the other side yet

TICKLER: Sniiiiiiiiiiiiiiiiiiiiiiiiiiiiiiiiiiiiiiiip

TICKLER: The final snip, dismantling them completely isn't bad

TICKLER: It's when I slowly pull them off you

TICKLER: Like they're melting off

TICKLER: And suddenly you're in boxers and bare legs

TICKLER: Your shirt comes off even quicker

TICKLER: Not only are you almost nude – you're not getting back to where you were before

TICKLER: And that's when my too-warm, too-moist tongue lands on your right nipple

TICKLER: And swirls that thing around

TICKLER: Licking, lapping

TICKLER: Flicking the tip

TICKLER: My finger flips the other one

TICKLER: And fuck is it hot

TICKLER: Moist nipple versus flicked nipple

TICKLER: Teasingly

VICTIM: duuuuuuuude this prep is the most torturous thing I've ever imagined being done to me

VICTIM: keep going

TICKLER: Then, slowly, the fingers begin moving

TICKLER: And your armpits are nervous

TICKLER: Shivering

TICKLER: But they can't escape

TICKLER: The fingers, twitchy and hungry for tickles, descend

TICKLER: They enter the pits themselves…

TICKLER: And wiggle

TICKLER: They tug on each nerve ending

TICKLER: They scratch each centimeter of skin

TICKLER: They twist those pit hairs around

TICKLER: And you'll be fucked if you aren't laughing your head off

TICKLER: Over and over

TICKLER: It's not the tickling

TICKLER: It's the CONSTANT tickling

TICKLER: Each side is equally bad

TICKLER: You try twisting to one side or another but you can't.

TICKLER: Your pits are a tickler's delight

TICKLER: The fingers are massaging

TICKLER: Scratching

VICTIM: :s

TICKLER: Truly, obsessively fondling your tickle holes

TICKLER: The index fingers are now making wide traces of nothing but the outside of your pits

TICKLER: And somehow that's worse

TICKLER: They're crawling up your biceps

TICKLER: "The tickly, tickly spiders, crawl up the water spout…"

TICKLER: They quickly tease your neck

TICKLER: Fondle your ears

TICKLER: My gods, you're ticklish all over

TICKLER: Then that mouth descends on the other nipple, the dry, flicked one

TICKLER: And now it's getting really moist, really fast

TICKLER: Some teeth are brought in just to switch up textures

TICKLER: No biting, just evil, evil play

TICKLER: And poor you, in your poor boxers

TICKLER: You got that little open slit in the middle of your boxers

TICKLER: And there's no button

TICKLER: And your embarrassed, horny, exposed member has snuck on out.

VICTIM: *shivers*

TICKLER: Precum right on the top of its head

TICKLER: You pray I don't notice, but it's too late, I have

TICKLER: I slowly grab the base

TICKLER: One pump…

TICKLER: TWO pumps…

TICKLER: And it stops

TICKLER: *SNAP*

TICKLER: A photo is taken

TICKLER: Oh horny boy, of all the times to be horny, why now, in front of my camera?

TICKLER: That shit'll haunt you later

VICTIM: lol

TICKLER: And then I bring out "Softie"

TICKLER: The softest, lightest feather in the world

TICKLER: Not really good for armpits

TICKLER: Dragging through toes maybe, but you still got your ankle socks on

TICKLER: Oh no

TICKLER: Softie has another mission

TICKLER: Softie wants to slowly glide along one side of your shaft

TICKLER: The left side

TICKLER: Once

TICKLER: Then twice

TICKLER: And then a third time

TICKLER: But… only on the left side.

TICKLER: Not the right

TICKLER: It feels good but… why won't I just drag it along the right side, just once, pretty please?

TICKLER: But I ignore you

TICKLER: Only one side of your shaft is being tickled by Softie

TICKLER: Softie's having a blast over there

TICKLER: Your right side isn't

TICKLER: It tickles but fuck this is frustrating

TICKLER: Now Softie has found something it likes:

TICKLER: The lip of your cockhead

TICKLER: That too-sensitive area right underneath the mushroom, right at the tip of your shaft

TICKLER: Softie likes playing in there

TICKLER: Teasing

TICKLER: Dancing,

TICKLER: Tickling.

VICTIM: wow

TICKLER: TICK-LE-ING

TICKLER: And suddenly you are your cock head

TICKLER: Sometimes your cock twitches with pleasure when just the right areas are feathered

TICKLER: Your whole will is being broken by a feather named Softie

VICTIM: I'd be spurting a lot of precum dude

VICTIM: believe me

TICKLER: Oh I know

TICKLER: Embarrassingly so

VICTIM: yep

TICKLER: Which is exactly what Softie wants…

TICKLER: It wants to tease you

TICKLER: It wants you HORNY

TICKLER: It wants your helmet redder than it's ever been

TICKLER: It wants you not spurting precum – it wants a stream of it

TICKLER: And all Softie has to do is dance along the lip of cockhead

TICKLER: Your cock is now filled with nothing but tingles

TICKLER: Those fuzzy tickles right before you orgasm

VICTIM: yeah

TICKLER: Tingly, tingly, and tingly in your cock

TICKLER: Tingly tingly, tingly

TICKLER: Softie is having a field day

TICKLER: And then, right when tingly has almost etched a pump-a-thon out of you… it stops

TICKLER: And nothing happens

TICKLER: Nothing.

TICKLER: You hear me go grab something

TICKLER: And then you hear me standing on the bed

TICKLER: And then nothing

TICKLER: Again

TICKLER: A whole minute passes

TICKLER: And then it starts:

TICKLER: The lotion

TICKLER: First one drop lands on your shaft

TICKLER: Then another right next to it, on your stomach

VICTIM: ohhhhhhhhhhhhhhhhhhhhhhhhh

TICKLER: And then it starts streaming

TICKLER: A lot of it is just pouring down

TICKLER: It's covering your cock

TICKLER: And your balls

TICKLER: And especially your too-sensitive cockhead

TICKLER: In fact, it's getting messy, there's so much lotion there.

TICKLER: But fuck, it feels SO GOOD

TICKLER: Then you feel my bare foot line itself up with your cock

TICKLER: My big toe traces the front of your shaft all the way to the rim of the cockhead

TICKLER: And then wiggles back and forth on the front of it

TICKLER: And your tickling fetish converges with your foot fetish

TICKLER: A sexy bare foot is touching your horny member

TICKLER: Your horny member absolutely covered in soft, fluid lotion

TICKLER: It feels like everything wonderful and sexy in the world at once

TICKLER: And you cum hard

TICKLER: But there is so much lotion, your shots are dampened, and it just mixes in

TICKLER: Like it's contained

TICKLER: Like the glog has caught you

TICKLER: Which is frustrating, 'cos you want to feel your hot cum all over your neck

TICKLER: But instead, this MASSIVE orgasm just pulls near your navel

TICKLER: Gobs of cum meets an ocean of lotion

TICKLER: And suddenly your horny cock is FUCKING SENSITIVE TO EVERYTHING

VICTIM: *shivers*

TICKLER: At which point you feel my finger circle the elastics of your ankle socks again… and you realized that your body is more sensitive than ever… and those socks haven't even come off yet…

TICKLER: ;-)

VICTIM: noooooooooooo way lol

TICKLER: >:D

CHAPTER SEVEN

THE HYPNOTIST

A lot of sex, when you get right down to it, is about control. While people talk about dom/sub aspects of sex all the time, what they're doing is talking about control, either being in control or being 100% not in control. That's why bondage tends to be a turn-on for some people as well, because once you're immobile, you are at the complete whims of the person who has restrained you. Trust is always important in those cases, and when done right, everyone is beyond happy by the end. Same thing goes with hypnosis as well: it's almost like bondage for the mind, and the thing to note is that no one can ever be force-hypnotized – everyone has to be willing from the get-go (that's why stage hypnotists always ask for volunteers, never forcing an audience member on stage, 'cos it flat-out won't work). As such, I figured that in order to get what somebody truly wants, a round of hypnosis just might do the trick one of these days...

"He is so fucked."

"What do you mean?" asked Andrew, eyes on the videotape in Hypnotist's hands. Instead of answering, Hypnotist simply shot back a smirk – one that let him know that all will be shown in good time.

Andrew genuinely wanted to know what was going to happen to Simon. After all, Simon provided the basis for Andrew's entire curriculum: he was the ultimate victim. Simon's life was completely in the hands of Hypnotist, and the best part was that Simon didn't even know. Simon had been Hypnotist's mental slave for the better part of a year, and as such, Hypnotist could get whatever he wanted from Simon. Given that Hypnotist was already one horny motherfucker, this meant that Simon was at Hypnotist's beck and call every week, humiliating himself offering up his body for Hypnotist's every devious desire, every fetishistic fantasy, and every orgasm that Hypnotist wanted to have. The best part though? Simon never left with any memory of what transpired…

This kind of control over someone – over every aspect of their body – was exactly what Andrew wanted. Andrew was a handsome guy in his early 20s, with lightly tanned skin and short brown hair that swooped like a GQ cover models would (heck, if Andrew ever got over his affinity for t-shirts and Chuck Taylors, he probably WOULD get a modeling job if he wanted). This, coupled with his effervescent smile, naturally made Andrew a lightning rod for female attention. He had his first major makeout session when he was 16, and had sex just two years later. The girl behind both of these events, Raquel, was long out of the picture by the time Andrew got to college.

Yet even with the inventive prom invites he got showered with year after year (and Facebook friend requests from girls he didn't ever recall meeting), Andrew had gradually come to the conclusion that he wasn't really into relationships with girls. All the chick flick movies with those predictable plots, enduring long car rides with Katy Perry blasting out of the speakers, all this wildly unnecessary pillow talk AFTER sex – it wasn't his thing. He liked rock music, action movies, and sports games. He liked to see things get crushed and egos get bruised. In essence, he liked power on display. On campus, he never joined a Frat but he spent every waking moment he could at one;

drinking games, hyperbolic tales of sexual conquests, collectively yelling at a plasma TV screen when the Raiders fumbled – this was more Andrew's speed.

And then came Seth.

For a while now, Andrew had been taking into account the way his Frat friends behaved: overly macho, domineering, yet – weirdly vulnerable. Always wearing shorts and sandals, not backing away too much when talking about "feelings" – it was odd. The shorts and sandals thing was also interesting to Andrew: a guy being barefoot is in and of itself an unusual thing – a sight that was more meant for girlfriends and wives; a state of undress. So for a group of guys to be too together and partially naked, exposed – well that piqued Andrew's interest. When groups of them wrestled for no reason and one unlucky soul wound up calling uncle because one guy discovered his ribs (or worse, his bare soles) were ticklish – that worked too. Andrew wanted that: to experience doing that to someone – but Andrew tended to be rather shy. Andrew knew that if he went up to one of his baseball cap-wearing pals and asked to play with their feet, he knew their innate homophobia would kick in and he'd be ostracized in nanoseconds. He didn't feel safe about asking anyone to do it – until he met Seth.

Seth worked at the campus eatery (the official school one that hires students for abysmal wages), and goddamn was he witty. Seth – with his blonde short hair, deep blue eyes, and slight bit of pudge in his shape – was one of the nicest, most efficient cafe servers you could imagine, capable of whipping together a dirty chai and a cooked pizza pretzel in what seemed like 90 seconds. Given Andrew's weak spot for strawberry smoothies (and only them), Andrew wound up visiting the campus eatery a lot. Through his upbeat and joke-filled chats with Seth, Andrew gradually began making what he considered his first "true" friendship in college, despite being a senior. The two began hanging out after Seth's shifts, and gradually more so on weekends. Seth was a gigantic sci-fi nerd but you'd never guess it by looking at him: most sci-fi nerds were never that witty or outgoing. Fun was had, drinks were shared. Yet there was one small aspect about Seth's life that Andrew never really understood: Seth never went barefoot anywhere. This wasn't a topic that came up very often, but in all honesty, that small facet didn't even matter: the bond between the two guys was strong, almost sacred…

…Which is exactly why Seth was Andrew's number one target. He wanted to rip off those shoes and socks and have a party with his favorite nerd's feet. He wanted to hogtie him his all-black (by requirement) work clothes and see how he reacts to constant, diabolical tickling. With his gorgeous looks, Andrew still got advances from girls all the time, but taking that road would be far too easy; Seth was someone who he couldn't have in any circumstances – which is why he wanted him all the more.

But how?

He couldn't trick Seth into doing this, nor could he really explore the inner lurkings of Seth's sexuality (Seth already had a girlfriend, whom Andrew quite liked actually). There had to be some other way, and that's when it stuck him: Hypnotist.

Andrew's attraction to guy's feet was a bit off kilter – he knew that – but he just couldn't get enough of that macho vulnerability. There were tons of videos on YouTube of guys literally just taking their socks off on camera and wiggling their toes around. Those (usually face-unseen) guys just KNEW that people were getting off on their bare feet, and that mixture of vulnerability and swaggering machismo only intrigued Andrew further. Yet what took the cake was a mysterious user known only as Hypnotist. The guy would simply set a camera down as he sat down with his friends and put them in a trance.

Hypnotist couldn't have been older than 28 – slender, confident, a perfectly wry and devious smile – but his mastery of the art of hypnosis was unparalleled. He'd have nerdy guys think they were honest-to-goodness puppy dogs in one video, sassy lingerie models in the next. The instant rapport he had with his victims was incredible. The "deepness" of the victim's trance states was amazing. And this is why a bulk of Hypnotist's videos were about his own fetishes, which were eerily parallel to Andrew's. One video featured a burly, overweight college quarterback – light traces of a beard intact – sitting down on an old couch in an old yellow T-shirt, jeans, and soccer cleats. Hypnotist cued him into thinking that whenever he said "tickle" the guy would get a little bit hornier. In this video, the QB was just melting into the cushions of the couch, snoozing away in his deep trance. Hypnotist would say "tickle" – evenly, very matter-of-fact – and suddenly QB's back arched ever-so-slightly. A subconscious smile spread across the chubby college athlete's face, and every time Andrew saw that grin, he got excited. That was not a run-of-the-mill smile, no: that was a smile that belonged to a boy experiencing extreme pleasure deep down in his soul. Hypnotist would say "tickle" again, and QB just giggled. Hypnotist said it yet again, and what started as a giggle slowly turned into a moan. QB's hips thrust unconsciously – in three utterances QB was probably fully erect. THAT was power. THAT was control. THAT was vulnerability. And suddenly, Andrew found his in with Seth.

Of course, YouTube doesn't allow nudity, and Hypnotist's videos ended before getting to "the good stuff", popping up a link to his video site at the end. Andrew memorized each and every preview – especially of the lacrosse athlete who was under the idea that removing his socks and feeling the air between his toes would get him instantly hard – and once even bought one of "The Confession", wherein a nerdy computer programmer type who, under hypnotic suggestion, unearthed every male-male sexual encounter he had. It was extra devious because Hypnotist prompted him with the idea that the deeper the secret was, the hornier he would get. Needless to say, it was Andrew's most watched DVD by far (easily displacing *Boondock Saints*).

These videos sent a series of devious thoughts into Andrew's gorgeous head.

Unfortunately, that made nights hanging out with Seth all the more awkward. Seth didn't pick up on any of Andrew's secret desires – to him; he was just having a good time with a friend. Andrew was too, but not without those devious ulterior motives. Even when they went out to a nearby bar on the hottest day of the year so far (highs in the low 80s), Seth's dress remained unchanged: long pants, comfortable sneakers, shin-length white cotton socks. Not a sandal in sight. Even when Andrew dropped some foot-related topic into conversation, Seth rarely addressed it. These actions were driving

Andrew slowly out of his mind. Now he didn't want to ruin a good friendship, but was he really so bad for at least wanting to take a peek at what he wanted?

Later that night, laying in his too-small dorm bed and staring at the ceiling, Andrew made his decision: he was going to contact Hypnotist.

Andrew was a little hesitant at first – after all, he was just about to ask an online hypnotist to teach him how to control his friend for sexual pleasure – but he didn't see any other option. He sent off a simple private message to Hypnotist's YouTube account, thinking nothing would happen (guy must get 1000 e-mails a day, right?). Much to his surprise, he got a message back within 10 minutes. After reviewing Andrew's description of the situation, Hypnotist was intrigued, and thought he could help. He asked where Andrew lived, indicating that he lived… in the same city where Andrew was going to college? Holy crap. Andrew didn't really believe in fate, but this came pretty damn close…

After exchanging a few messages back and forth, the two decided to meet up at Hypnotist's place, which he claimed was an upscale studio apartment downtown. The day of the meet, Andrew threw on his Birkenstocks and cargo shorts and drove on down to Hypnotist's address. When Andrew pulled up to it, it was obvious that Hypnotist was not lying about his digs. It was an apartment obviously meant for people making over $100,000 a year. Andrew nervously went in and made his way up to Hypnotist's apartment. The door looked like it was made of solid oak. Andrew was sweating a bit nervously, but knocked on the door. This was a mistake right? Meeting up with someone just 'cos of their YouTube videos, right?

The door opened. The man opening it was as handsome as could be: dirty blonde hair, blue jeans, wearing an unbuttoned black dress shirt over a regular black T-shirt and featuring a smile that was almost as flashy as Andrew's. He extended his hand: "You must be Andrew."

Andrew smiled back, and shook hands. "Guess I must be."

"Come on in, make yourself at home." Hypnotist shot a quick glance down to Andrew's feet. "Nice sandals." Andrew blushed a bit, but didn't know why.

Hypnotist's place was gorgeous: gigantic glass windows giving an overview of the whole city, hardwood floors, and what appeared to be a fully-functional bar in the middle of the place. Andrew looked in awe, but was most in awe of his host: damn that guy was attractive. If only he wasn't wearing black socks...

"Beer, Andrew?"

"Um, sure?"

"Heh, most people would just say Blue Moon instead."

"Not Miller Light?"

"Andrew, do I look like a dirt-poor frat boy wannabe?"

Andrew smiled – he didn't know who this guy really was, but his forceful flirtation was kind of fun. Hypnotist noticed this, but didn't play into Andrew's obvious shyness. Instead he asked the best ice breaker question he possibly could: "So, friend, why don't we get things started by having you sit down and tell me what you want to do to Seth..."

For the next hour, the two chatted about the foot-shy Seth, the way that masculine vulnerability got Andrew off, and Andrew's many fantasy scenarios. This, in turn, lead to a long discussion about hypnosis, and shocking no one, Hypnotist knew a lot about the practice. The first lesson that Hypnotist gave was a very important one: that the only way people could be hypnotized was if they actually wanted to be. Those cartoons about people being hypnotized against their will by villainous gangsters were not factually accurate. Secondly, you couldn't physically touch the victim in the trance, except under very rare circumstances. You could convince a victim to take off their socks, sure, but to then drag your fingernails across their soles, it could break them out of the trance (and really freak them out to boot). Lastly, the level of trust the victim had with his master was key: the stronger that was, the deeper the trance could go. Hypnotist explained this all very elegantly, as Andrew ate up every last word.

That first session turned into weekly meetings, and before long Hypnotist had Andrew trying out certain exercises, doing research back in his dorm, and viewing even more hypnosis videos (including some naughty ones that didn't even make Hypnotist's website). On the duo's seventh meet up, Hypnotist wanted to show Andrew "something incredible." No, Hypnotist didn't want to put Andrew through his own session or two like he did last time. Instead, all Andrew would do is watch a video…

"What is it?" Andrew asked, toes curling in his sandals, eager and curious.

"It's a video I made of Simon – the best victim anyone could ever have. He's the basis of your entire curriculum. To put it another way: he was my Seth, and the stuff I got him to do was pretty amazing."

"So what happened?"

"Well, let's put it this way, Andrew: he is so fucked."

"What do you mean?"

Hypnotist smirked, the tape of a session with Simon twirling in his hands. He didn't have to say anything to his excited pupil at this point: he just popped the tape in his VCR player, and watched a tale he knew all too well…

———————

The tape flickered to life, and it was… a surprisingly normal scene. A plain light yellow couch in someone's house, a small table in front of it, and a guy sitting right there on the couch, alert and active. Andrew deduced that this was Simon. He had a bit of a baby face and a schoolboy haircut, but donned a light green Legend of Zelda t-shirt and light tan cargo pants. Not traditionally handsome, but not bad by any degree. Hypnotist was speaking off camera.

"Alright, you ready there, Simon?"

"Oh sure, man. And you're SURE this will cure me of my insomnia right?"

"Hypnosis is capable of some pretty amazing things, man. The only reason it works is because the brain can cure the body of so many things without even trying: hypnosis just guides it to the right path, OK?"

"OK, man," replied Simon, very of matter-of-factly. "Just don't turn me into a chicken or anything."

"Heh, heh," cackled Hypnotist, "I wouldn't do anything like THAT to you."

Andrew looked at the real-life Hypnotist standing behind him, his face glowing in the light of his TV set. His smirk was unmistakable: he was really enjoying watching this again.

Hypnotist told Simon to close his eyes and lean his head back. The college-aged Zelda-lover did so. Hypnotist's voice took on an NPR-styled cadence: assuring yet unmistakable, confident and knowing. Andrew was already aware of Hypnotist's powerful speaking voice through the practice sessions they did in person, but to hear it confidently boom through a craggily old VHS was a bit surprising: no amount of distortion was preventing him from luring his victim even further down the rabbit hole.

After Hypnotist warmed Simon up by having him tense and relax his body with his eyes closed – one segment at a time – it was obvious that Simon wanted this to happen and was already feeling more relaxed. Hypnotist then went through his classic spiel…

"Alright Simon, now I want you to feel your body. I want you to really feel how relaxed it is. Every part of you is feeling more relaxed than it ever has before. You can only hear the sound of my voice. You cannot hear any other sound than that of my voice. You are now feeling your body sink into the couch and into the floor. Deeper and deeper, deeper and deeper. The deeper you go, the more you go into a sleeping state, where the only thing you hear and respond to is my voice. Deeper and deeper, sleepier and sleepier. You have never felt so relaxed in your life. The more relaxed you become, the more prominent my voice echoes in your mind. Deeper and deeper, sleepier and sleepier. The deeper you get, the deeper you want to go. The deeper you go, the more my voice reaches out to you, like a lasso reaching into your soul, capable of pulling you out of your slumber at any second. You want to thank me for guiding you with my voice, and you thank me by going deeper and deeper, deeper and deeper. Now when I count to three and snap my fingers, you will fall under my complete command, addressing me only as 'sir', each word I say driving you deeper and deeper, deeper and deeper. Now 1, 2, 3…"

Hypnotist snapped his fingers, and Simon – who looked like he was being completely enveloped by the couch cushion and dangerously close to being absorbed by it – slowly rose, Lazarus-like, until he was sitting perfectly upright. Even on the slightly-grainy VHS tape, Andrew could see Simon's eyes stare ahead, blankly and without emotion, never once blinking. Andrew had seen hypnosis videos, but not like this. This… was intense.

"Now Simon, what do you hear?"

"Only the sound of your voice, sir."

"What do you want to do?"

"Obey your commands so I can go into a deeper state of sleep, sir."

"Good boy, Simon. I will reward you now by telling you to go deeper and deeper, deeper and deeper."

Andrew watched as Simon slowly blinked his eyes once, as if to acknowledge Hypnotist's command. As eerie as the whole viewing experience was, Andrew felt like he was opening up a whole Pandora's Box of erotic delight just by watching this.

"Now Simon, you like jerking off, correct?"

"Yes, sir."

"Do you like it when you've teased out your cock to the point where it's positively dripping with precum, right? To the point where every tingle it feels just might be the one that sends it over the edge, right?"

"Yes, sir. Very much so."

"'Very much so,' ay? Well that's quite impressive young man. That is why you are going to be turned on like you never have been before, Simon. Lie back onto the couch for me."

Simon did so, sitting much like the way he did before.

"Alright," began Hypnotist, a devious tenor slipping into his voice. "I now want you to place your feet on this table in front of you."

Simon did so. He was wearing generic light-brown sneakers with white laces, and what looked to be – just like Seth – shin-high ankle socks. The position of the camera made it so Andrew was looking right at the bottoms of Simon's sneakers. Already, the anticipation of what was going to happen was killing him – he had barely even noticed he was already fully erect...

"Now," started Hypnotist, relishing every word, "you are a horny young boy. What I want you to do now is wiggle your toes around inside your shoes. Yes. Can you feel those toes trapped in the canvas of your shoe? Constricted in those white cotton socks? Oh, how wonderful it must feel to remove those things. So wonderful, in fact, that whenever you get barefoot, you get turned on. To feel air circling your toes, to bend and flex them freely – that idea of liberation is a huge turn on to you, and right now you want nothing more than for that to happen."

Already, Andrew could see in the video that Simon was squirming. His feet flexed back and forth on the table and an unconscious, deep smile and snuck its way onto his face. Dude seemed like he really, really wanted to be barefoot. This was remarkable.

"Now Simon," continued Hypnotist, "what do you want right now more than anything?"

"To be barefoot, sir." A tinge of horniness was creeping into Simon's voice.

"Would you get horny if I untied your laces right now?"

"Yes sir!"

"Good..."

Suddenly, a slightly younger-looking Hypnotist crept on camera, and he fondled the tops of Simon's sneakers, obviously savoring each and every detail. The more the fingers danced over the tops of those laces, the more Simon could be seen squirming. Slowly, Hypnotist began untying the laces of Simon's right shoe, loosened up the tongue, and then grabbed the shoe by the heel and ever-so-slowly peeled the shoe off; exposing Simon's socked sole to the camera. By the time it was completely off, Simon's right hand had already snuck its way down to his crotch, unconsciously stroking his manhood with a very obvious sense of purpose. Although Hypnotist's head was out of frame, it was obvious that he was smiling.

"I'm going to do the next shoe now," he started again, "and the more the shoe comes off, the deeper you fall into your state of sleep – and the hornier you get."

"Yes sir," Simon said, practically moaning it.

The process was very similar for the other shoe, except Simon was enjoying it even more now, his grin so wide it could almost be called stupid-happy. As Simon's left shoe came off, Simon started to moan – this was practically sex for him. All ten toes subconsciously flexed with their newfound freedom, his hand still stroking his cock through the front of his cargo pants.

Hypnotist paced around his sock footed victim, soaking it all in. "Now, Simon, you like stroking your manhood, don't you?"

"Yes sir."

"Unzip your pants and start pumping."

Casually, Simon proceeded to do so. The unzipping was slow, very deliberate. Simon didn't even drop his pants far at all. He just pulled out his wide, cut cock and proceeded to rhythmically pump away, his eyes now closed and ears waiting anxiously for instruction.

"Alright Simon – three things are now going to happen. First, with every pump you take, you are going to fall deeper and deeper into your trance state. Secondly, even as you approach a climax, you are not going to cum until I order you so. Understood?"

"Yes sir," moaned the unconscious masturbator. God, he was not stopping now was he?

"And last but not least," intoned Hypnotist, "you are REALLY going to enjoy this next part…"

With that, Hypnotist hooked his fingers around the rim of Simon's right sock and pulled it down past the ankle and around the heel of the boy's foot. He then stopped: most of the sock was now scrunched up around the middle of Simon's sole, while the part near the toes was straight and untouched. Simon kept pumping at regular intervals. Hypnotist now grabbed the tip of Simon's sock – right between the big and first toe – and began to slowly, slowly pull the sock from Simon's foot. As he did this – with the fabric slowly running past the ball of Simon's foot – Simon's moaning was pitching up gradually higher. Before long the rim of the sock made its way over the toes, though Hypnotist just left it dangling there, like a cotton bell with Simon's toes as the hammer. This teasing only increased Simon's pitch.

Hypnotist then did the same with the other sock, and Simon's moaning got even worse.

Finally, after doing the bell bit with Simon's left toes, the boy was splayed out and completely barefoot. His toes freely wiggled and the pumping began to slowly increase. A high pitched whimper followed – goddamn the boy was horny.

"Stop!" Hypnotist declared – and that's exactly what Simon did. No complaints, no nothing: dude flat out halted mid-pump. Simon's pre-cum-stained hand went immediately to his side, like it was his default position. What a well-trained boy Hypnotist had on his hands there.

"Now Simon," started the master, "do you like being barefoot?"

Simon's voice shot up like a child on Christmas morning: "Fuck yes, I love it!"

"Good boy. Now, I am going to start licking your beautiful, amazing-looking feet here now. With each moist molecule that lands on your soles, you're going to get hornier and hornier, hornier and hornier. If you shoot, that's fine. As I lick, you are going to verbally thank me, and with each thank you, you fall deeper and deeper into your state of sleep. Understand?"

"Yes sir!"

Hypnotist went down to his knees. He sniffed Simon's left foot very deeply, and already the boy began to moan. Then Hypnotist's tongue slowly stretched out, starting with Simon's thick heel and then gradually inching up the boy's exposed sole. As he did so, Simon's high pitched whimper came back, hips unconsciously thrusting, no hand anywhere near his cock. Hypnotist continued this on the other foot, slowly dragging his wet tongue from Simon's thick heel to sensitive sole to ball of his foot to base of his toes. Once there, Hypnotist slowly engulfed some toes in his mouth, and then it happened...

Without even having his cock touched in any way, Simon shot off a rocket of cum, accompanied by a high pitched squeal of pleasure. The rockets came again and again and again. Hypnotist got him good. Simon's whole body was almost shuddering through the whole thing, from initial launch to the dozens of small aftershots. It was a sight to behold.

A pause filled the air. Simon's eyes were still closed. Hypnotist went over to his hypnotized victim and tucked the boy's beet-red cock away, zipping him all up but leaving the cum stains as is. He then paced around for a bit.

"Did you enjoy yourself, Simon?"

"Yes sir," said the boy, very flatly.

"Good. Again, with each word of my voice, you get deeper and deeper, deeper and deeper. Now, when I snap my fingers, you are going to wake up, but two things are going to happen. First off, in your daily life, you are going to become bored with shoes. And socks. You'll wear them for a week or so, but then socks are going to feel uncomfortable, and unnecessary. You'll buy cheap plastic flip-flops and wear them whenever you can. You'll take good care of your feet, and they'll take on a new prominence to you. Understood?"

"Yes sir."

"Then repeat it back to me."

Much to Andrew's amazement, he did, almost verbatim. The slave's mind was almost a steel trap now: it truly absorbed EVERYTHING that Hypnotist said.

"Very good," continued Hypnotist. "Now, one more thing. You will now have a trigger installed in you. You want to hear this trigger more than anything in the world. Anytime you hear the phrase 'footslave', you will instantly fall into the state of trance you are in now. You will respond to only my voice, and only I can set you to 'normal'. And you will get hornier with each lick of your bare, exposed feet. Understood?"

"Yes sir."

"Then repeat it back to me."

Again he did.

"Good boy, Simon. Now when I snap my fingers, you will wake up and have absolutely no memory of what happened. Understood?"

"Yes sir."

"3… 2… 1…"

He snapped, and Simon's eyes went big, blinking a lot as he looked around the room with a confused look on his face, totally not catching the fact that his cock was out and exposed.

"Hey man," started Hypnotist, "I was worried about ya. Fell asleep there for a bit. You OK?"

"I guess," stated the boy, "I just… where are my shoes?"

"Dude," intoned Hypnotist, "what happened to your shirt?"

Simon looked at the numerous cumstains and was aghast. He saw his dick hanging out there in the open and immediately tucked it back in his pants, stammering for an explanation.

"I… I don't… it's just…"

"FOOTSLAVE!" Hypnotist yelled, and Simon collapsed in the couch all over again, happily snoozing and awaiting commands.

Hypnotist cackled a bit, and then turned the camera off. The video was done.

———————

Andrew, who's cock was practically ripping through his shorts, looked up at Hypnotist, who was grinning at his star pupil.

"So…what'd you think?"

"I… I'm amazed. The stuff you did broke so many of your own rules…"

"I know, Andrew, but this was about the 20th time I had put him under. This was the first time, however, that I really got to get what I wanted. You work with your victim enough, focusing on building that bridge of trust and control, and you can do whatever you want with them… just like you'll do with Seth."

"That's great!" said Andrew, smiling. Yet slowly, his smile turned into a look of concern. "There is just one thing that concerned me, though."

"What's that?"

"Those 'triggers' you gave him. I mean, once you start messing with people's subconscious, that stuff gets really freaky. I mean, what if you alter their personality for the rest of their lives? Doesn't that, ya know, bug you or something?"

"It's a moral gray area, yes, but it's got its perks."

"I… I don't know," started Andrew, hesitantly. "That's just… I don't know if I want to be a part of that aspect of it. I'm sorry."

"Oh Andrew," said Hypnotist in a reassuring tone, "there's no need to apologize at all. Besides, you're already involved in that part of it whether you like it or not."

"What do you mean?"

Hypnotist placed his arms around the seated Andrew and softly whispered those two deadly words into his ear: "Tickle Toy."

Just like that, the trigger that Hypnotist placed in the boy's brain during their last "practice" session went off, and Andrew completely collapsed in his chair, held strongly in Hypnotist's arms. He whispered again: "You ready to be tickled until you cum, Andrew?"

The hypnotized boy responded "Yes, sir."

Hypnotist smiled again, because he knew this was going to be one hell of a night…

CHAPTER EIGHT

THE NAUGHTY PROFESSOR

I literally have the best friends in the world. When I told my close friends that I had a book of erotica out, they didn't laugh or mock my slightly-unusual fetish, no. Instead, they were amazed <u>for</u> me, so happy I could get a book published, and several even going as far as to buying it (and asking me to sign it as well). Although virtually no one has read it (save one of my closest friends, who did, which lead to a hilariously awkward conversation afterwards), that kind of support means a lot. One of my friends from home, Jamie, in talking about the book, went as far as to ask if he could be written into a book. What were the restrictions? None. I could do literally whatever I wanted to him in this tale. As such, I took those words to heart, and well, Jamie, here are just a few of the unbelievably naughty things that I'd do to you...

The young professor was sweating, because for the first time in a long time, he felt genuinely nervous.

Jamie had stood up there before facing a sea of dead fish eyes before, lecturing and engaging about everything from Moliere to Ayn Rand (it was his own damn curriculum after all), but he knew that in the end, he gets through to these college freshmen. It showed in the test scores. After all, he wasn't too far removed from their wavelengths. He himself was in his early 20s, with dark straight hair, glasses, and a generally casual teaching ensemble, oft-accentuated by his solid black flip-flops, giving off a vibe of liberal-arts cool while still being able to reach out to his students about current pop culture and use it as a tool instead of a feigned attempt at education. He knew, for example, that using *The Matrix* as a "jumping off point" in a discussion was pretty pointless these days, as its cool factor had long-since disappeared (and, with each new class that came in, fewer and fewer kids had seen it).

What was making today unusual, however, was not the fact that he was trying to engage the kids about Rand's *Anthem*, figuring the shortest work would be the easiest for the kids to penetrate (it wasn't). No, what was making him nervous was the man who was auditing the class. A tall, slender fellow who was right around Jamie's age, if not a year older. He wore jeans, a plain white T-shirt, and some ratty green Chuck Taylors from gods knows when. His hair was black and short, his gaze piercing. What was making Jamie nervous was not the fact that this handsome guy was sitting in his classroom; it was that he was looking at Jamie the whole time. When Jamie told everyone to reference a page in the book or when everyone's heads turned to face whichever student was trying to articulate Rand's views on capitalism (rather unsuccessfully, Jamie might add), this mysterious man's eyes were still staring intently at Jamie. Every once in a while, those eyes would drift down to Jamie's sandaled feet, eyeing the curvature of each and every toe, which, for whatever reason, made Jamie extremely uncomfortable. His own toes would sometimes curl, as is shying away from the stranger's penetrating gaze. What was troubling Jamie the most was that this mystery man was smiling the whole time, eyeing him like he was some sort of snack or prey or something. Whatever this man was looking at, it was obvious that he was enjoying what he was seeing.

The bell rang, and it caught Jamie off guard. He hurriedly reminded everyone about starting Conrad's *The Heart of Darkness* next week, and went back to his desk to organize his papers. Out of the corner of his eye he watched his visitor approach, and calmly turned around. Jamie cleared his throat a bit.

"Hmm, I'm sorry... I don't think I caught your name, sir." Jamie felt strangely nervous even asking this.

"Name's William. And you're Jamie, right?"

"Why, yes. Um, yes." Jamie was wondering why he was getting so flustered.

"Good talk today, Jamie. I enjoy Rand."

"Heh, that goes more than I can say for a lot of my students. I hate her, personally."

"Aww, that's a shame. Ain't nothing like being reminded that each person's achievements should remain with them and only them for the rest of their life."

"Well, ya know, sometimes something should be given up for the greater good," Jamie intoned.

"Oh? And when was the last time you gave up something of yours for the greater good?"

"Um... what do you mean?"

William just smiled. "Sounds like you need to give a good sacrifice, Jamie. Sounds like you need to maybe even try something new. This job... it's got you down, doesn't it?"

Jamie was a bit taken back by how forward this guy was, and went on the defense. "Um, I'm sorry: you're studying for what degree?"

William snorted a bit. "Nice try, Jamie. I'll be a Flounders tonight at 9PM. See you there."

"Um, listen, I..." – Jamie was trying hard to say something back, but William simply walked straight out the door to the classroom without even looking back. What a cocky bastard, Jamie thought. Also, what... what an unusual exchange. Who says that to someone? What the hell was he even talking about? Jamie tried shaking the exchange out of his mind. He's got papers to grade tonight anyways. At least he's got a funny story to tell people later, right?

It was 8:25PM, and Jamie wasn't getting anything done. He was sitting on his couch, clothes unchanged from class earlier, a stack of papers right on his credenza. Beer in hand, he had just finished another disc of the latest season of *Family Guy* that he bought, having only graded two papers in the past three hours, and even then he kind of half-assed it (a "B" grade is a good indicator that he only skimmed it). He swirled the half-sip left in his beer bottle, and got back to staring back into space a bit, his mind pre-occupied. Try as he might, he simply couldn't get that conversation out of his mind. What the hell was William talking about? In truth, Jamie was a bit appalled that this guy would just say "Flounders, 9PM" and just expect him to show up at that popular campus bar. It was presumptuous, bold, and pretty damn arrogant. Sure, Jamie could be that arrogant himself sometimes, but this – this was different. This was pointed. It wasn't like the guy ran into Jamie by accident, no. It's like Jamie had been selected, targeted even. And that conversation – it was just lingering with some ulterior motive. Jamie didn't want to know what it was… but, at the same time, couldn't help himself. Last thing he wanted to do was to go to Flounders to meet up with some stranger; after all, that would mean that he is simply playing into this guy's schemes. This was a scheme, right? People don't just say "Flounders, 9PM" to people like that, right? No, of course not. They'd have to want something from him. But what?

Jamie's head was becoming a traffic-jam of too many thoughts. He set his beer down and vowed not to think about it for the rest of the night.

He revised that deal 10 minutes later, saying he'd see if he couldn't find out some information about the student later on to get behind whatever was going on.

A bit of time passed. Jamie looked at his phone: 8:50PM. He was lightly buzzed from the beer, but only lightly. "Fuck it," he said, grabbing his flip-flops and heading for the door. It was May, he was near the end of the term, and he was goddamn curious. What had he to lose?

———————

Jamie got to Flounders around 9:05PM. It was a Thursday night, so it wasn't packed, but had a couple of students from college littered about. Jamie had been there once or twice, which was a bit unusual: student teachers are told not to "fraternize" with the students themselves, but his occasional hush-hush appearances only added to Jamie's on-campus "cool" factor. He had already got reports back that some girls in his previous classes had developed crushes on the bespectacled young lad, which he honestly kind of enjoyed hearing about – nothing wrong with being considered sexy.

Tonight, however, he didn't run into many students that he himself knew – just some young'ns that he knew in passing. There, staked out at the bar, was William, sipping on a beer whilst staring at the TV, some random hockey game going on. William hadn't changed his attire at all, and Jamie found it odd: who wears plain white T-shirts these days? Jamie tried scanning the room to find some place to go to wherein he could eye William from a distance and then see if he reacts and moves towards him – but fuck it. Jamie took the barstool right next to him.

"Hey there," Jamie started.

William turned to face him. "You're late, Jamie."

"Heh, I'm curious. I'm not late, just curious."

"Curious about what?" A grin crept over William's face as he spoke.

"I... I don't know. It's just, rarely do I..."

"What you having, Jamie?"

"Oh, I already drank tonight. Um... a cranberry juice is just..."

William had already started waving down the bartender: "Hey! Two vodka and tonics? Thanks."

"Listen, vodka doesn't really..."

"Trust me, Jamie; you're going to enjoy it."

Jamie eyed William with cautious eyes. "You seem to be taking an unusual amount of interest in the life of a student teacher."

"And you seem to be taking an unusual amount of interest in someone who audited your class only one time."

"Well, you started the conversation, William."

"Yes, I did, Jamie. You got me. Maybe I just wanted to talk to you about Ayn Rand more: did you ever think about that?"

"Oh god, I hope not."

"Heh," snorted William, "if that were the case, I know you wouldn't have showed up. You hate Ayn Rand, remember?"

The drinks had arrived. Jamie, strangely, took his right away and took a sip before responding, "Yes, yes I do."

"Good." William took a sip of his drink as well. "So why are you here?"

"'cos you invited me."

"No, no, no – that's not good enough, Jamie. I'm a stranger – you don't know me. And, judging by the dripping cynicism in your lecture today, I take it you're a bit of an introvert as well. You don't like people much, do you?"

"Well, largely because most people are dumb."

"Heh, I'll drink to that." Both men clinked glasses and sipped again. William donned that sly grin again: "So why are you here?"

"I… I don't know. I was curious, I guess."

"Curious as to what?"

Jamie paused for a second, and then sipped once more. Already, he was feeling a bit more buzzed. "I don't know that… something might happen."

"Like what, Jamie?"

"Like… I don't know. Something unexpected. Something fun, maybe."

"Heh, heh, let me get this straight: you went on a whim to meet a guy at a bar who you barely know for 'something fun'? That's pretty crazy."

"Well, hey, dude, if you're not going to…"

"Oh no, Jamie. I'm impressed. I just want you to realize something: you don't just go to a bar thinking that 'something fun' might happen. You go 'cos, perhaps deep down, you WANT 'something fun' to happen. Did you ever think about that?"

Jamie took a large sip. "OK, and if I said 'let's do something fun', what would happen?"

William's smile just grew larger. "There's a whole world you don't even know about, Jamie. I'll only show you if you want to try something genuinely new."

"Something... naughty?" Jamie literally couldn't believe that just came out of his mouth.

"Oh, it's definitely naughty."

Jamie started to get up. "Well I'm out, then. I got a girlfriend, thank you."

William calmly placed his arm on Jamie's shoulder "No, no, it's not like that. We know you have a girlfriend. In fact, we think you're one of the straightest guys we know."

Jamie was back to sitting. "We?"

"Never mind that now. Jamie, your girlfriend is out of town this weekend, right?"

Jamie was a bit flabbergasted. "I, uh... yes, but, how did you know..."

"What if I told you there was a way for you to orgasm that would be unlike anything you've ever experienced before?"

What a bold declaration.

Jamie cleared his throat. "Again, I'm not gay, and I don't..."

"Jamie," William started, "let me tell you about human sexuality. You've probably seen what I've seen: straight guys. Gay guys. Every hesitant stage in-between. Yet I want you to find me a gay guy who doesn't have a nice set of lady friends and is just slightly, remotely flirtatious with them. I want you to find me a guy who is married with three kids who hasn't once roughhoused with his frat brothers and had at least one random, drunken moment of stupidity. Jamie, people can get pretty set in their ways, completely closing themselves off to other experiences, sometimes consciously, and sometimes not. Yet when you're facing a glory hole and you're getting your knob worked over quite nicely, I don't think the gender on the other end really matters."

"Listen, I…"

William placed his hand on Jamie's shoulder. "Jamie, if you come with me right now, I will give you the most earth-shattering orgasm you've ever had. And you know what the best part is? You won't have to have sex with a guy, you won't have to have sex with a girl that's not your girlfriend, and your junk will remain untouched by anyone's mouth."

Jamie paused, the alcohol definitely hitting him. "And… I'd still have the best orgasm of my life?"

"Oh yes."

Jamie thought for a second. He thought of his empty apartment. He thought of the 20+ papers sitting there that remained ungraded. He thought about how often he had refreshed XTube this week alone. He stared at that gin and tonic, and then just thought "Fuck it." He downed the rest of his drink and turned to William.

"Lead me away."

William smiled. "Right this way, professor…"

William made some signal to the bartender then lead Jamie through a door near the back of the bar. They walked through the kitchen and eventually made their way to a set of stairs leading to a basement underneath the bar. The stairs were wooden and a wee bit creepy, but fuck it: what's the worst that could happen?

———————

William unlocked some heavy wooden door underneath the bar and let Jamie in. "Welcome, Jamie." Jamie looked around: it was pretty barren. There were about four rooms down here, all connected by open doorways. In one room was what appeared to be some bright lights, but William lead Jamie away from there, taking him to a room where many comfy seats and sofas were, small fridges in-between each one.

"Beer, Jamie?"

"Um… sure," he said, plopping himself down on one of the big comfy chairs. "Quite the get up you have here."

"I know," said William, handing Jamie a Blue Moon from one of the mini-fridges next to Jamie's seat. He pulled a footrest in front of Jamie. "Listen, make yourself at home for a bit – you have to meet someone else."

"Um… OK" said Jamie, twisting off the bottle cap with his shirt. He slipped his flip-flops off and placed his big bare feet on the footrest in front of him, then swigging the beer. Man, he was being treated well tonight, all things considered. Then, William came back into the room, this time with another guy. He was a bit taller than William, about 200lbs: some weight but no girth. The man had a light bit of beard slapped on his face but had a nice blue button-down shirt that he was wearing.

"This," William started, "is my friend Andy."

Andy went over to shake the reclined Jamie's hand "Pleasure to meet you, Jamie."

"Likewise."

The two men then sat down on chairs next to Jamie. There was a slight bit of nervous tension in the air. Jamie was curious.

"So… what am I doing here?" Jamie asked, before swigging another bit of beer.

"Well," started Andy, "there's been kind of a running thing amidst students here on campus. A running gag, as it were: who is the hottest teacher."

"A gag?" asked Jamie.

"Well, more like a poll," continued Andy, "a 'light-hearted' poll. And, well, for two years now, you've kind of come out on top."

Jamie smiled a bit. "Really?"

"Oh yeah," continued Andy, "and, well, some people kind of write in their fantasy scenarios about what they'd want to do to those teachers, and…"

"Like what?"

Andy stammered a bit – he was obviously nowhere near as confident as William. "Well, it varies from person to person, really."

"Tell me one."

"Well, there's one about wanting to worship your manly, powerful feet."

"Heh, worship? Like, sucking on toes and the like?"

"Yes."

"And whose would that be?"

Andy's head dropped a little bit. "Well, um, that would be mine, actually."

Jamie snickered a bit, fascinated. "Really?"

"Yes, sir."

Jamie wiggled his toes, slowly, right there on the footrest. "This doin' it for ya?"

Andy's body lightly shuddered. "God, yes."

Jamie took another swig of beer. "Then have at it."

Andy took a quick glance over to William, who simply nodded in approval. Andy immediately got down to his knees, and drew his face to mere inches away from Jamie's toes. Andy took a big, visible inhale. He shuddered again, this time with raw pleasure. He brought his nose up to the base of Jamie's toes, and inhaled again. Then, without even second-guessing, his mouth slowly enveloped Jamie's big left toe. Jamie hadn't felt anything quite like it: it was so soft and warm. It... kind of felt good. Slowly, the mouth began moving on to other toes, and Christ-be-damned Jamie kind of liked it. The guy was pretty much making out with his feet there, which was unusual, sure, but feeling that warm tongue slither between this toes – kind of a soft, private area – it... yeah, it felt pretty good. Of course Jamie didn't want to show it – he was mainly having fun. He took more swigs from his Blue Moon, and by the time he was done with one bottle, William had another at the ready for him. Jamie kind of got into this whole "being treated like a king" thing, rubbing one foot through Andy's hair while the other's toes were being swallowed passionately. Andy alternated regularly, soon taking to licking the entire bared sole, sometimes chewing on his heel a bit (which made Jamie laugh – it tickled, kind of). The drunker Jamie was getting, the more he was enjoying it. Jamie didn't even notice the fact that William was sitting right next to him, simply watching and observing the whole thing, absorbing details like some devilish sponge. Once Jamie began moaning a bit, William knew he had him.

William gestured to Andy to stop, but Jamie wasn't done having fun.

"Bet your mouth tastes like my feet, don't they, boy?"

Andy stood up, doing his best to hide his erection through his dress pants. "Yes sir, that's about right."

William spoke up: "Enjoy that, Jamie?"

"You know what," Jamie started, before swigging once more, "I kind of did. However, that did not get me off, I must say."

"Heh, that was just a fun little diversion, Jamie. If you really, really want to experience that orgasm, then we need you to go one step further."

Jamie swigged again, and then burped a bit. "And... what might that entail?"

William pulled a blindfold out of his pocket. He placed it carefully between Jamie's big and index toe, still lightly moist with Andy's saliva.

"If you want to know, strip down to your boxers and put that on, and I'll guide you the rest of the way." William and Andy began slowly walking out towards the room where all the bright light was coming from. "And if not, the door's right behind you." Then, just like that, the men were gone.

Jamie sat alone in the darkness, his feet relaxed and his third beer mostly empty. Even if he left right now, he'd still be drunk, happy, and have one hell of a goddamn story to tell. Then again, he thought of how his girlfriend was out of town, how much he didn't want to grade those papers, and was already buzzin' – why the hell not, right? He got to his feet and stripped off his shirt and pants. He was wearing his blue-checkered boxers, which were kind of a favorite of his. He got to putting on his blindfold, before stopping to yell "Do you want the flip-flops on or off?" Andy yelled back "On, please!" Jamie's feet slowly scooched into place on them, his toes aligning with the sweat-stained imprint of his feet from years of wear. He then made sure the blindfold was snug and secure. "Ready!" he shouted, before standing upright and tall, bravely facing a completely unknowable future. He heard someone come into the room, and then grab both his hands to lead him into the room where the bright light was. "Don't worry," said William's voice, "this is where the fun begins."

———————

Even with the firm blindfold on, Jamie could still tell he was being lead into the bright room. It was a bigger room too, as the sound of his sandals slapping against his bare heels echoed much more here than in the other room. The lights kept getting brighter, and eventually William stopped him, and turned him around.

"OK now Jamie, there's a wall behind you. I'm going to press you against it, OK?"

"Um, OK."

William pressed lightly on Jamie's chest and sure enough, there was a wall right behind him. Felt like there were things connected to it. William positioned Jamie's arms in… a strange position, like a referee's touchdown. Then, William used his sneakered feet to spread Jamie's legs a bit so they were a bit more than shoulder-length apart. Jamie found it odd, but kept cool (he was a bit drunk, after all). Then William whispered in Jamie's ear: "You ready for this?"

Jamie simply said, "Why not?"

Suddenly, both William and Andy's hands were on him, and… he was being restrained. The wall he was up against was apparently covered in hospital "safe" restraints, his arms and wrists being strapped into that referee "touchdown" position quite firmly. Same happened with his spread legs: a series of leather straps holding him very tightly into place. He found it odd that there were straps right over his inner thighs and above his hips – they wanted that pelvis kept completely in place for some reason. Jamie didn't fight it at all. He just drunkenly smirked a bit and said "OK boys: what's next?"

"Heh," William smirked. "This."

The fingers descended on Jamie's bound body – and they wanted to tickle. Fingernails and fingertips and all sorts of wiggling digits were scooping the inside of his armpits, finding the fleshy bits in-between each rib, and squeezing his inner thighs. This kind of attack took Jamie completely by surprise, but instead of gasping out a profanity, he just quick-shifted into deep, stuttering laughter. His flesh had suddenly turned into tickle meat, and those finger vultures were fuckin' hungry. A finger traced the circumference of his tummy; another one was rubbing his nipple between its thumb and index finger, while another was dancing along his bicep. Having four hands doing all these things at once before abruptly alternating elsewhere – Jamie had never felt anything like it. He was fighting as hard as he could, but he was completely restrained, the occasional armpit-hair scrape still causing his arm to try to jolt inward, but, of course, it was completely unable to. His body was experiencing excitement and frustration at the same time, and it was driving him nuts.

The armpit thing was really driving him the most insane, as that is such a sensitive area that all you want to do is just close it off to tickle attacks but here were two pairs of hands using completely different patterns on each one, swirling the armpit hairs around, tugging on them lightly, dancing right up against the spin, and goddamn they tickled. If he could struggle just a bit he might be able to offset the sensations, but he had no choice: his body had to accept the tickles, and goddamn do the tickles tickle. Jamie tried fighting the laughter, but he was hopelessly outmatched: they were conjuring these giggles out of him so damn well. Jamie was a tickle puppet, and there were two people pulling his strings. He could almost hear them say "Dance, puppet, dance!" and he had to whether he liked it or not.

Then, the tickling stopped, and suddenly his nipples had two warm, moist mouths hovering over them. The tongues extended and began flicking the very tip of his nips over and over again. Having his nips being licked by two mouths at the same time was an absolutely unreal feeling. He fought them as much as he could, but the boys were doing the smart thing by winning over his nervous system before they did his mind. Jamie had wanted to yell at his captors for so long during the tickling, but now – they were just trying to get him aroused. The moist, wet tongues still flicked and licked, the occasional hand began feeling or squeezing Jamie's inner thighs. All the while, Jamie, against his will, was getting a little hard. He tried moving his hips but he had no choice: a small tent began to form in front of his captors and their many bright lights. Jamie fought it, trying to think of un-sexy things or thinking of some witty retort, but those tongues were practically lapping at the pleasure centers of his brain now. He got harder and harder, and before long he was at full mast. A hand soon came down and slowly opened up the small "button hole" in the front of Jamie's boxers, allowing his erect manhood to slide through. That same hand then slowly wrapped its fingers around Jamie's cock and began pumping away. Soon, feeling his cock get jacked like that while having his thighs squeezed and his nips licked wildly, all of this mixing with a light state of drunken ecstasy, well, it didn't take long before the tingles on Jamie's tip took hold and he shot out a respectable load, his cock eagerly rocketing out streams of cum for everyone to see. Soon, it stopped, the hand pumping gradually slowed down, and the tongues retreated. The sweaty, blindfolded young student teacher began to pant, sagging in his tight wall restraints.

Jamie couldn't see anything but heard William and Andy milling about the space. Some mechanical things were moving about – not, like, machines, but small devices. He would've asked questions but was panting too hard.

"So," William intoned, "how'd you like it?"

"Well," Jamie began between bucket breaths, "it was… surprising."

"Surprising is good."

"Yes," he panted again, "but you promised me… the best orgasm of my life."

Jamie could practically hear William smirking. "I know. Some water?"

"Fuck yes."

William held a water bottle to Jamie's lips and gradually tipped it upwards. "There ya go, boy. Drink it up." Jamie, like a dehydrated hamster, glugged away, practically emptying the whole bottle in about 20 seconds. A quiet silence came over the entire room.

"So," Jamie started, "are you guys going to let me down or what?"

Jamie could hear the sound of chairs being pulled up right next to him. "Not yet," started William. "Remember, we promised to give you the best orgasm of your life, and that's a promise we intend to fulfill."

Just like that, Jamie felt a hand hold his boxers still. Then came the snipping of scissors, and just like that, Jamie was completely naked (save the flip-flops), strapped standing next to a giant wall. His cock, however, was completely spent.

"Well," chortled Jamie, "I don't know how to break this to you guys, but I honestly don't think I have another one in me. I mean, thank you and everything, but – I'm pretty sure Mr. Muscle is done for the night."

"Heh, heh, heh," laughed William, "we're going to have to disagree with you on that."

Jamie was growing nervous. William continued:

"Jamie, did you know that when you mash up two pills of Viagra and mix them into a regular run-of-the-mill water bottle filled with tap water and feed it to a student teacher strapped to a wall, it is practically tasteless?"

Even underneath the blindfold, Jamie's eyes got huge.

"Oh no you fuckin' don't! Let me out of this fuckin' thing!"

"Jamie, even if we do, it's already going to happen – and you're going to be hard for a while."

Suddenly, Jamie felt it. Despite feeling like he couldn't get hard for another hour, the stiffening began, and he fought it as best as he could, moving his body around as much as he could in the tight restraints, trying to shake off that energy to somewhere else, but he couldn't help it. Slowly, he had a yearning erection. It was stiff at first, but it felt like it kept growing, like his cock was just straining to shoot out of his pelvis. Gods, Jamie had never been this hard in his life, and the worst part was that he didn't even want to be.

Then, Jamie heard William and Andy repositioning themselves on either side of him, both sitting down in chairs, his cock probably about eye-level to them. Then, he felt it: a feather on his left side. It slowly glided from right underneath his cockhead to the base, and then back again. Then, another feather did the same on the right side, and FUCK IT TICKLED. His cock twitched, but that's all it could do: twitch with pleasure while it got teased. Jamie's hips went into a wild dance to try and get away, but they could barely move – the feathers were having a lot of fun teasing the sides of his cock. One stroke up, one stroke down. One stroke up, one stroke down. It was unnerving. Jamie could feel tingles start to form, but couldn't do anything but just feel them grow greater in strength.

Jamie's mouth tried to articulate a proper "FUCK YOU!", but all that came out was dribbling horny nonsense. The feathers then took a breather, and then one snuck behind and scraped the underside of his balls. Jamie yelped at the touch, and it's right as then that the other feather scraped the frontside of his mighty cock, focusing specifically on the space between the middle of his shaft and right where his cockhead started, that sensitive area where it tingles the most. Jamie angrily growled the best he could, but his cock told a different story, once again twitching with pleasure at such torment. This was insanity, and the worst part was that Jamie knew he wouldn't be going soft for a long, long time. His hard cock was suddenly his captors' playtoy. Jamie growled again, but this time in frustration over the fact that his cock was no longer under his control.

This epic feather-tickling continued for about ten minutes but what felt like an eternity to the still-bound, still sandal-clad, still-sweating Jamie. Then William proclaimed, "Finally! Pre-cum!" Jamie's cock was starting to lightly ooze its clear, sticky liquid, a sign that it was enjoying what was happening to it far too much. The feathers still continued their light scraping of his most sensitive of areas, and at one point, one began lightly circling the tender rim of Jamie's cockhead, driving his rod absolutely bonkers. That small bead of precum soon became a small stream, and it was starting to leak onto the ground. Jamie wasn't making noises as much as he was random sounds now: partial giggles mixed with animal grunts, his cock torment becoming too much for his logical brain. The feathers stroked again. And again. Then, suddenly, they stopped.

"Now," said William, "watch this."

William placed his entire palm over Jamie's cockhead and began moving it around, gathering as much pre-cum as he could, soon smearing the rest of Jamie's entire cock, moistening the whole thing up with his own jices. It took a second for Jamie to realize what was going on, but then he realized what was happening: once his whole cock was moist, it was that much more sensitive to everything around it. This was evidenced by William and Andy taking turns blowing on the sides of Jamie's cock, seeing if the motion of the air in the room was enough to make it go into a pleasure twitch. Amazingly, it was, and the tingles of excitement and frustration were practically bursting out of Jamie's body. He had never, ever, ever been tormented like this, and his mind was imploding upon itself.

Two hours passed.

Jamie's cock was now deep red, practically throbbing from its torment. William and Andy had gotten it to the point where a single feather stroke made Jamie's cock twitch twice and stream that much more pre-cum. It was begging, begging for release. A minute passed. Another light feather stroke. Another involuntary pleasure twitch. Jamie wanted to rip this wall in half, but couldn't. All he could do was twitch. Jamie was almost in horny tears by this point – he had never been tormented for this long.

William then spoke to his victim, "How you feeling, boy?"

"PLEASE!" Jamie started, "I need to cum! I need to cum so bad!"

"We know. But, what will you give us in order for you to cum?"

"FUCK! ANYTHING! ANYTHING YOU WANT! JUST LET ME FUCKING CUM ALREADY!"

"Will you let me keep your sweaty sandals?" asked Andy.

"YES!" screamed Jamie. "You can have all my footwear! Anytime! Just let me cum!"

"Do you give us permission to release a videotape of you?"

"WHAT?!"

"Well, we blindfolded you so that you wouldn't see the video camera that we're filming this. We figure that this would not only be great blackmail, but a fun way of luring you back to us for even more fun in the future, don't you think?"

"You can't do that! That's illegal! That's just –"

A feather stroked his cock, and it twitched again.

"You gonna cum for me, boy?" said William.

Jamie whimpered his reply: "Puh-lease! I need, need, need to cum!"

"Going to let us release the video?"

"Nooooooooooooooooooooooo…"

Another feather stroke. His cock happily twitched away once more, and Jamie snapped.

"RELEASE IT GODDAMN IT LET ME CUM!"

"And let us play with your feet immediately after you cum?" asked Andy.

"MY FEET ARE YOUR TOYS NOW! JUST LET ME CUM!"

"As you wish," said William.

Jamie felt not one, but two feathers at the base of his cock. The lightly danced upward, along his shaft, toward his cockhead, and then…

"FUCCCCCKKKKKKKKKKKK!"

Jamie didn't just cum: he exploded. Rockets of cum shot out of him. The first one gigantic, the second one almost comparable. Streams of cum came pouring out, one after another, each rocket pump making his tip even more sensitive than before. By the seventh, eight pump, Jamie's cock had gotten too sensitive, and each involuntary pump after made him cringe.

"Goddammit! Stop! Stop cumming you fuck!" he shouted to his manhood. Finally, the pumps died down, and Jamie's body practically collapsed in his own restraints. Before long, his mind went with it, and he passed out.

———————————

Jamie's alarm went off, and he groggily moved his exhausted body. He looked up: 8AM. He had class in an hour, but every inch of his body completely ached. His cock especially. He thought back to last night – was that real? Did that even happen? He didn't want to go to school, but he had students to teach and educate and fuckgoddammit he felt like shit. He had never felt so exhausted in his life, and he once ran a marathon.

As Jamie forced himself up, he looked for his flip-flops, but they were absolutely nowhere to be found. Instead of breaking out the sneakers though, he just got some soccer slides that he had but never wore. Putting them on with his usual teacher ensemble, they definitely felt weird.

He got into class around 9:10AM, already late. He walked immediately to his desk, and then looked at his class: it was filled with students he didn't know. Oh sure, everyone he normally taught was in their desk, but it was standing room only: about two dozen guys were there, none with a pen or paper to take notes on, all eyes on their professor. Then it dawned on Jamie: they were here to "audit" him. He slowly, carefully walked in front of his desk and leaned against it. He scrunched his toes in his soccer slides, and saw all those auditors take a collective gasp.

With that, Jamie's suspicions were confirmed: he was completely fucked.

CHAPTER NINE

THE ROOMMATE

There is a story that I could write but probably never, ever will. It's that of what happened with me and my roommate my junior year of college. I was kind of falling for the guy, and he was extremely straight and, worse, one of my closest friends. I didn't want to damage the friendship, but it lead to awkward moments on my end (many, in fact). I still loved his feet like mad, however, and occasionally would get the chance to suck on his toes while he drunkenly slept. Being an "alpha-male" all the way, I soon began playing the role of the victim, hating tickling and hating feet all the way, going out of my way to express my displeasure about either when I was being tickled by him or when he put a foot anywhere near my face. He used these things I despised to torment me even further, and before long, I had created one powerful tickle monster. Although the actual tale could probably fill up an entire book by itself, I wound up gravitating towards this slightly fictionalized version of things, as it covers a lot of the highlights of that year quite, quite nicely...

A single drop of water was all it took to change Cody's life forever.

This drop had landed on his forehead, and Cody slowly woke up, wondering what the hell was dripping water on his forehead. Right there, in the middle of the night, Cody's dorm room pipes were extracting revenge on him once again. For while Cody did have his bed right next to the window, his bed was also directly underneath a run of metal pipes (painted, of course, to match the bland walls of the room), and even after calling it in to campus maintenance, here he was, once again, awoken by a single drop of water, right in the dead of the night.

As Cody turned to his side, however, he noticed there was a light still on in the room. That was strange, he thought, given that when he and Alan went to bed, everything was completely turned off. Alan was one year older than Cody, but the two had become friends through various literary classes, as both shared a wicked sense of humor that soon bled over into movie nights, drinking nights, and much more. Alan, with his slight Italian heritage, bowl-cut black hair, and somewhat athletic inclination (well, if you consider Ultimate Frisbee supremely athletic), certainly had an attractive charm, less so his build, although he was still a catch for the ladies on campus. Cody, meanwhile, with his short, straight blonde hair and gawky frame, was less so a catch, even though he radiated creativity in virtually every class and endeavor he participated in. Perhaps Cody and Alan's friendship looked slightly odd on the outside, but on the inside, things were bubbling: while Cody was Alan's trusted confidant, it was Cody himself who actually harbored a bit of a crush on his older friend – and had an intense male foot fetish to boot.

Living with his object of desire and foot-lust was nothing short of heaven for Cody. When his roommate was gone, he could raid through Alan's laundry basket and find the dirtiest pair of socks he could possibly find, lying back in his bed (window blinds very obviously drawn) and inhaling every single molecule of foot stink there was, which, in turn, caused his hardon to rage like it never had before. Unlike most people in such a position though, Cody felt guilty about his urges taking over during those alone times, as he felt like he was being dishonest to his friend. Every once in a while, a paranoid delusion would race through his brain, like the one time he was licking the sweat blackened insoles of Alan's leather sandals, tasting each and every bit of Alan's foot that he could, before hearing the door to their dorm room be slowly unlocked, causing Cody to scramble back to his computer, wondering if Alan "figured it out" a few minutes later when he put his foot right in the sandal that Cody had just finished tonguing the living hell out of. Anytime a "close call" like this would happen, Cody would stop doing anything fetish-related for a few days (well, except maybe jack off to some of the images he had stored on his computer), out of both his fear of losing his friendship and for the fact that he couldn't help but feel that he might be slightly in over his head. Yet after a few days, Alan would come back from a brief jog, toss those white ankle-socks into the laundry hamper before taking a shower, and Cody's curiosity got the better of him. It wasn't his fault that the smell/taste of Alan's feet seemed to only get better and more pungent with each and every passing day…

Which brings us back to Cody and the Case of the Mysterious Light. After quietly looking around, Cody could see where the light was coming from. In their room, Alan and Cody's desks were placed together, creating a slight bit of a wall/private area for each roommate. Being standard-issue for a college campus, there was a backing to these desks, but not underneath where the students' legs were supposed to go: this was designed to make it so that they could more easily feed computer/printer/speaker cables through. Yet, when placed back to back, these desks allowed someone a perfect view of everything that was happening waist-down on the other side, like Cody for example. At this moment, what he was seeing was the dim blue light of Alan's laptop reflects across the young man's naked, horny body.

Yes indeed, at around 3AM that evening, Alan was sitting there at his computer, pantsless, slowly teasing and jerking his cock to who-knows-what. Although this didn't necessarily fit into Cody's "interests", he was nonetheless fascinated by what his roommate was doing. So confident in his own quick-jerk habits, it was fascinating to not only see someone else take his tender time in getting off, but also to see his closest friend do something so base – it cast him in a different light. His object of lust was no unintentional foot god – he was just another guy at a college who was horny like all the rest. Alan had some sort of lotion with him, and slowly, carefully worked his cock over, moistening it up every few minutes for maximum effect. Every once in a while it would involuntarily twitch, no doubt excited by something it had seen. Over 20 minutes, in the faintest of lights, Cody watched with absolute fascination, unable to tear his eyes away. When it came time to climaxing, a few quick sheets of tissue were brought out, and Alan's mighty shaft pumped away on its own, oozing out cum, undoubtedly satisfied with its accomplishment. Cody simply lay there awe-struck – he couldn't believe what he had just seen. He remained motionless as Alan went to the restroom to clean himself off, having just seen the most private of command performances.

As the weeks rolled on, Cody came to realize that this was actually a fairly regular event, and each one seemed to be more fascinating than the last. Cody always wondered why Alan took showers at night, but now that he was watching these too-private shows at night, he began to understand: ain't nothing like walking into your room with a bathrobe on, opening the front, and feeling like you're truly a king in your chair. One night, Alan even jerked it while still wearing his ankle socks, which fascinated Cody even further, seeing those toes, stretch and wiggle while hidden in a thin sheet of white fabric – it was proving hard for Cody to not jerk it in tandem. Of course, those very socks became even more fantastic jerking material for Cody later…

Gradually, Cody's own behavior was changing. He was staying up later, feigning sleep just in case Alan decided to attend to his more primal needs. Some nights this gambit paid off, sometimes he was up for hours on end for no reason. He still did his schoolwork and hung out with friends, but still couldn't help but wonder what new Alan-oriented fetish treats awaited him at home. One night, Cody got back from a friend's downtown birthday celebration (see: drinking), and stumbled in around 2AM, trying his darndest to be quiet. He got to his bed without turning on the lights in the room and quietly slipped into his pajama bottoms, but not before he began to register something he hadn't heard before: the sound of Alan snoring. Alan almost never snored, so he must've been hella out of it. Cody looked around the dark room, his head still swimming a bit, but his inhibitions largely... gone. He, being as drunk as he was, thought that crawling across the room would make less noise, and proceeded to get on all fours and walk slowly towards the foot of Alan's college-regulation bed. Being how it was the spring, there wasn't much need for covers, and lo and behold, sticking out barely over the edge of the bed (and right out of the one thin white cover that Alan used to cover himself with) was Alan's glorious bare right foot. In his kneeling position, Alan's foot was about eye-level with Cody. The snoring continued, almost echoing in Cody's mind. So Cody, feeling a bit more daring than usual, placed his nose just an inch away from the base of Alan's toes. He sniffed. Already, he could get a sense of Alan's delicious foot scent, and he had an instantaneous hardon. This was exactly, exactly what he wanted...

Emboldened and unquestionably horny, Cody decided to take things a step further. He leaned forward and pressed his nose right onto the base of those toes, and inhaled deeply. Within seconds, a newfound sexual energy surged through the horny college boy, and if he hadn't been dripping precum before, he certainly was now. His left hand unconsciously began stroking his cock through his pajama fabric, knowing full well that he was in a state of total wrongdoing and total ecstasy all mixed together. That left hand began to start jerking his cock through the fabric, and before he knew it, Cody's soft mouth reached out for Alan's unconscious, helpless toes; starting by lightly sucking on Alan's pinkie toe, and then the one right next to that and onward until he was simply sucking on Alan's big toes in an very passionate fashion. The taste of Alan's foot sweat positively delighted Cody's taste buds, which, in turn, seemed to be connected directly to his raging rock, which twitched in approval. Cody took one more wet slurp of Alan's toes, and just like that, rockets of cum shot out his cock, making the entire front of pajama pants moist with hot sperm. Even after the final shot, tingles of pleasure continued to dance around Cody's entire body, and he could even feel this event get burned into his memory – this was an event he wouldn't forget anytime soon.

Once his body came down from its horny high, the kneeling Cody suddenly felt even more exhausted than before. He took one last glance at Alan's saliva-coated foot sticking out from the bed sheet, and after he heard one deeper snore, drunkenly crawled on all fours once again back to his bed, where he promptly passed out.

When Cody awoke, it was around 2PM, and he realized it was Saturday. This upset Cody, as that was the day that he and Alan had mutually agreed would be their "dorm room cleaning day". It was a bother (especially for Cody, who wasn't the cleanest of undergrads), but needed to be done for the sake of Mutual Roommate Sanity (or, as they oft referred to it, "MRS"). A quick look around showed that Alan was not around – perhaps he was studying or at a rehearsal for something – Cody could never remember which. So, after having a small bit of cereal from the duo's shared mini-fridge and changing into a dirty old T-shirt and his shin-high white socks (he kept his long pajama pants on though – they were just too comfy), Cody got to work wiping the dust off of their computer monitors and TV, doing a quick wash of the inside of their window (lord knows he wasn't going to go outside), and after checking his e-mail, went back to bed wondering what movie he'd lay back and watch this evening, soon dozing off while getting lost in his own thoughts.

Cody could hear faint bits of voices as he woke up, only to realize that it was yet another *Family Guy* DVD that Alan had put in the TV (that seemed to be what the TV was used for about 80% of the time). The 'mates chatted about their respective days with a relative lack of interesting detail – it was typically droll behavior for two guys who had been living together for all of four months. Alan asked how it was taking care of the "MRS", and Cody said it was fine – he got his cleaning done. Alan – in dirty white cotton ankle socks, cargo shorts, and green T-shirt from his Ultimate Frisbee team – kneeled to the ground for a split-second, looking across the room towards Cody's bed.

"Well, from here, I can even see some dust bunnies underneath your bed."

Cody, still on his bed, groaned. "Oh, but I did everything else!"

"A rule's a rule, man. I'm doin' my part tonight."

"But Alan…"

"Jeez! You could've done it by now instead of just yammering at me!"

Cody knew it had to be done, but conceived of the laziest way possible to do it. Without getting up from his bed, he reached over to his desk to grab some Swiffer wipes he had, and then rolled over on his stomach, squeezing his arm between the side of his bed and the wall, blindly using the Swiffer to grab whatever bunnies might be hopping around under his bed. During this process, his right leg was also seeping into that crack between the bed and the wall. No, this was not the most efficient position for cleaning things, but Cody didn't really care at this point – at least he didn't have to get out of bed. Well, technically, his feet were beyond the foot of his bed, but whatever: he was horizontal, and that was all that mattered.

Then, just as he was reaching for something he thought seemed like significant bunny, the weight of his leg and arm seeping between that crease between the bed and the wall gave way, and the bed pushed out from the wall just a bit, causing Cody to fall through the crack. It was very sudden and very loud.

Alan called over: "Are you OK, man?"

"Yeah," said the grounded Cody, figuring out what just happened. The bed only gave way a bit, but the rest of his body slipped through the crack between the bed and the wall (having an unbelievably gawky frame no doubt helped with this). His right foot, however, was still wedged in pretty tight between the foot of his bed and the wall – trapping it. He tried maneuvering his socked foot in every which way, but nothing happened.

"Hey Alan?"

"Yes?"

"Could you help me out?"

"What happened?"

"I'm… I'm stuck."

This warranted Alan getting up from his bed and walking over to his roommate's bed, and as soon as he saw Cody's predicament, he began to laugh wildly: Cody was completely trapped under his own bed, with one foot trapped between the wall and the bed. This… was comedy gold for him. Cody was less amused.

"How stupid are you?!" bellowed Alan, laughing hysterically.

"Alright, alright," started his trapped roommate. "Can you please just help push the bed to the side so that I can get out?"

"Aww, but how else can I play with your trapped foot like that?"

"OK dude," started a visibly panicked Cody, "no time for games. Just move the fuckin' thing, OK?"

Alan nodded, and said, "Sure… but I just got to do one thing first…"

With that, Alan walked over to the foot of Cody's bed and plopped himself down, cross-legged, in front of Cody's trapped foot.

"Hey Cody."

"Yes?"

"Are you ticklish?"

Cody's eyes widened considerably.

"DON'T FUCKING TOUCH MY FOOT FOR A SINGLE GODDAMN SECOND."

"Oh, you mean like this?"

Alan ran his index finger from socked heel to socked toes, just seeing what kind of reaction it would elicit out from his roommate. Cody, trapped, watched his body quickly convulse and scream. "FUCK!" he cried, "I'm very ticklish there!"

"Oh, really?" said Alan with a shit-eating grin. One more swipe of that index finger from heel to toe – Cody convulsed again. This made Alan smile quite a bit – he was enjoying this.

"Please," started Cody, "just stop. You had your fun, I just… please stop. I am so ticklish."

"Oh I know," said Alan. "That's what I'm enjoying the most. I'm just curious about what other reactions we can elicit out of you…"

Alan took all the fingernails of his right hand and began scratching up and down on the part of Cody's foot where the sole meets the heel, and Cody proceeded to fly into more of a hysterical fit than before. Laughter shook out of him, sometimes in cut-off bits and pieces. He tried protesting, but his words were choked by laughter, and so all that emerged from his mouth was a stream of delirious nonsense. All Alan had to do was scratch that foot just a bit, and it sent his roommate up the wall. He then grabbed the rim of Cody's sock and pulled it down and straight off. "Now, let's see if you're any more ticklish without the sock…"

Cody was about to scream but Alan's too-perfect fingernails were already at work on the base of Cody's toes, scratching and poking and prodding Cody's foot flesh. What should also be noted about Cody is that this is a guy who, despite his own fetish, does not really find much fun or joy in being barefoot himself, so houses his dogs in shoes and socks almost perpetually. What that means, however, is that his feet are unbelievably soft, so while fingernails across bare soles would be torture for some people, it was a living hell for Cody, and Alan's fingernails were practically ripping his nerve system in half with their ticklish touch. Some people describe certain sensations in a way that they're going to "jump out of their skin", but for Cody, it wasn't a metaphor: he honest to goodness felt like that was what was going to happen to him as Alan deviously played with his foot.

Twenty minutes passed.

There was Alan, tickling Cody's bare foot with the same effort and vigor as twenty minutes ago, and there was Cody, trapped under his own bed, sweating, weak, and leaking out rambling half-laughs all while Alan used his fingers to trace the sides of Cody's foot, which was making him blather even more. Finally, after what felt like three hours for Cody, the tickling stopped. Alan stood up and moved Cody's bed a bit so that he could free his tortured foot. Almost instinctively, Cody curled himself up into a ball, his barefoot rubbing next to his socked one, as if one was comforting the other. His ordeal was over, and all he wanted to do was pass out into unconsciousness right then and there.

He then felt Alan grab his leg and begin to pull him out from under the bed. "C'mon boy, we ain't done yet." In any other circumstances, Cody would resist and fight, but here, exhausted from excessive tickle torture, he couldn't do a thing. Alan pulled the boy's full body out and splayed him face down on the floor, but positioned

Cody's feet on either side of the corner post of his bed. Alan then grabbed one of his belts and tied those feet together behind the post very tightly. Even though Cody had no strength to do anything, things were obviously about to get very real…

Alan then helped Cody get to his knees, which was tough given his feet were bound behind the bed post. Once he was fully rigid though, Alan then took Cody's hands straight up over his head, like a prayer that turned into a backbend, and once his hands were past the wooden bar that kept both bedposts together, Alan used another belt he had to tie Cody's hands together. He then stood back to look at his masterpiece of bondage: there was Cody, kneeling, hands tied above and behind him, leaving his ribs and armpits perilously exposed.

What's worse, Alan then pulled over the chair from his desk and placed himself just inches away from Cody's bound body. Cody, still exhausted, thought that perhaps this was all just one big nightmare he was going through.

Alan really enjoyed seeing his prey all-helpless like this. "It's kind of cute, actually."

"What?"

"You all tied up and ticklish like this."

"Fine, just get it over with," started Cody, hoping some reverse-psychology would do the trick.

"Oh no, we're going to do something even better than that, Cody."

"Um…"

Slowly, Alan's wiggling fingers descended towards Cody's ribs.

"Tell me Cody… what's the password for your computer?"

"YOU'RE NOT GETTING MY PASSWORD!"

"Oh, but I think I am, Cody…"

The first few fingers fell right onto Cody's left side, and then his right shortly after. Cody's face grimaced and turned, doing everything it could to not break out into a smile.

"Tickle, tickle…" Alan was saying this in the most teasingly evil voice Cody could imagine, and it was weirdly making him even more ticklish, enhancing the feeling of those fingernails poking and dragging across each and every rib, setting his nervous system on fire and driving nothing but tickles into his brain. Tickles was all he could think about and yet he was doing everything he could to stop them. The corners of his mouth drew up as if operated by strings and yet he couldn't stop. Bits of giggles emerged here and there, but this – coupled with the way that Cody's eyes were so firmly closed – it was obvious that his twisted face was holding back an ocean of laughter. This egged Alan on even more, as he felt that this was a new challenge for him. He alternated his strokes; he wiggled his finger around in Cody's belly button, and then did something new: his fingers dived right into the center of Cody's armpits, wiggling and tickling the whole way.

Cody practically exploded in laughter. He couldn't stop. The pits tickled like all fuckout. These were deep, wildly unhinged laughs. While tickling obviously causes involuntary laughter, these new pit tickles were causing said laughter to be wildly unhinged, as is if Alan was conjuring up some sort of great tickle spirit and Cody was the unwilling vessel. Cody couldn't even think straight – his brain was just nothing but tickles.

"Tickle, tickle, Cody. Tickle, tickle!" Alan loved the taunting almost as much as the tickling itself. "What's the password?" he'd ask on occasion, and just as Cody began forming the words "fuck you", his pits would be tickle-assaulted again, as Alan was single-minded in getting an answer from his newfound victim.

Finally, the tickling stopped. Cody's body sagged, slight aftershocks of laughter emerging every few seconds. Alan leaned back in his chair, content.

"OK, Cody, let's try this again. I am going to ask you for your password for your computer. You will tell me your password. Failure to tell me your password will result in a non-stop 20 minute tickle session. Even if you tell me your password during it, I won't stop. If you cannot say the password after that's over, then I'll give you yet another 20-minute tickle session. I'll keep doing this for as long as it takes to get your password. So, let me ask you one more time: what's your computer password?"

"Please," panted Cody, "Please don't make me say it…"

"Alright," started Alan, fingers primed for tickling, here we go again...

"NO! I'LL SAY IT! PLEASE DON'T TICKLE ME!"

"What is it, Cody?"

"It's... it's..."

"Yes?"

"Alantoes."

"... What?"

"The password is 'alantoes'."

Alan's eyebrow cocked, and looked real hard at his roommate, searching his face for answers. Silently, Alan stood up and went over to Cody's computer, sitting down and typing in the password. Windows made its little "welcome sound", and Cody, who couldn't see what Alan was looking out due to his position, still knew he was screwed. Alan began narrating his thought process out loud:

"You see Cody, I don't know about you. I see you getting drunk at parties and things but I never see you ask a girl out or even go on a date – and we've been living together for months. I don't see you flirting with guys, though, either, so – oh yes, right click – so I've just always been curious as to what porn DO you look at. I mean, if we're really going to..."

Alan was silent. All Cody could here was Alan clicking his mouse over and over and over again. A few minutes passed, but they felt like an eternity to Cody.

Alan then stood up and went over the chair that was placed right in front of the immobile Cody, sitting down and tapping his fingers on his knees.

"So... you got a foot fetish do you?"

"Well, it's not that simple, you see..."

"Oh no, I disagree Cody, I think it is that simple. Why else would there be close to a dozen photos of me barefoot in there? Some were even obviously taken while I was sleeping, one foot sticking out barely over the covers. Come to think of it, I think perhaps that is the reason that I sometimes am missing socks from my laundry. Maybe the machine isn't eating them – maybe you are."

"Alan, please, let me exp–"

"Oh no, that's fine, Cody, I think I can figured it out. Your password is 'alantoes' after all. You think my feet are goddamn sexy, don't you?"

"I... I don't want to..."

"Oh no, I think it's hilarious, Cody. Here, have a sample..."

With that, sitting in the chair, Alan rose up his socked feet and placed them square on Cody's face, the two feet practically enveloping him like a mask. "Sniff," Alan ordered. Cody didn't need any direction. Hell, he could practically smell them the second those socked feet were an inch from his face. In a few short moments those, those feet became Cody's entire world, and feeling them wiggle and move underneath a layer of cotton-sock fabric pressed to his face – it was bliss.

"This turn you on, Cody?"

Cody was unsure of what to answer in this case. "Well, I mean, it's a fetish, but..."

"Well I'm going to have to try harder, won't I?"

With that, Alan quickly slipped of his ankle socks and placed the base of his toes right underneath Cody's nose. "Sniff again."

"No..."

"Oh, you'll be kicking yourself later if you don't do this now, Cody. C'mon... give in... give in to the power of my feet..."

Cody struggled, trying not to show how much this was turning him on, but to feel that most foot flesh right against his upper lip, those feet radiating warmth as those toes wiggled – it was too much. A hardon began to form and began to press through his pajama pants.

"Well, well, well, looks like we have someone who wants to play."

Cody was beet-red with embarrassment, but there was nothing he could do: Alan, tormentor supreme, had found a secret way into Cody's horny fantasies, and there was not much he could do about it. All the while, Alan's meaty toes continued to wiggle on Cody's face, and his hardon twitched slightly underneath those pajama pants.

"Well Cody, it looks like you're obviously enjoying this. You've no doubt enjoyed looking at and playing with and taking pictures of my feet without my knowledge, so I think it's time I return the favor, don't you? Let's see just how embarrassed and horny you can get…"

With that, Alan took his feet off of Cody's face and grabbed the elastic edge of both Cody's pajama pants and the boxers underneath. In one swift move, he brought them right down to Cody's knees, exposing Cody's rock-hard, extremely red, precum-dripping circumcised cock, leaving it out in the open air of the duo's dorm room. Alan was living up to his promise: Cody had never felt more embarrassed in his life. Alan placed one of his feet right underneath Cody's balls, so he could feel this toes wiggle down there, and then placed the other foot right in front of his mouth, saying simply "Suck."

Cody had never been more of a slave to his own desires than right then and there. He slowly took Alan's toes into his mouth, and slathered his moist tongue around them, sucking on each one with relish, savoring every molecule of taste and every wiggle Alan could muster. All while this was happening, Alan was wiggling his toes gently underneath Cody's balls, and the two sensations together made for a delirious, insanely horny combination. In between toe-sucks, however, Cody caught a glance of Alan leaning back in his chair, eyes closed, stroking his cock through his shorts. It was a brief glance, but whatever Cody was doing to Alan's toes, it was obviously something very, very enjoyable…

Then, in one swift motion, Alan pressed his foot a bit further into Cody's mouth, allowing another toe to slowly sneak in to the warm, moist maw, and that was enough to send the boy off: Cody's cock shot off a gigantic cum rocket, landing almost entirely on Alan's hairy shin, which was then followed by another shot, and then a lesser one, and then a lesser one. Alan removed his foot from the boy's mouth and watched as Cody's body slowly came down from its horny high. Alan reached over and grabbed a new Swiffer cloth from Cody's desk to clean his shin with. He then got off the chair and kneeled down so that he was eye-level with Cody.

"Did you enjoy that?"

Cody was almost too weak to answer, but mustered out a faint "Yes."

"Good. Now, I have an unbelievably embarrassing story to tell about you."

"OK." Cody literally couldn't think of anything else to say.

Alan was shifting some thoughts around in his mind, and, surprising even himself, said, "Would you like to suck on my toes once a week?"

Cody felt it was a trap, but had to be honest: "Yes."

"OK. I will let you go, and you can suck on my tasty Alantoes for an entire hour every week… as long as you submit to an hour of bound tickle torture."

"Oh god, no!"

"No, you say? You would turn down the thought of my manly, tasty, tender toes dancing around your tongue just because you can't stand a little bit of tickling?"

"I… I…"

"This is a one-time offer, Cody…"

"Fine! I'll do it!"

"Good boy. Now rest up." Alan very unceremoniously undid the belts that were binding the boy to his bed, and as soon as they were gone, Cody simply fell to the carpeted dorm room floor and was asleep in seconds.

In the days that followed, he began running over the experience again and again in his head, and since the two carried on as if nothing happened, wondered if Alan was really going to live up to his end of the bargain…

… then again, it wasn't until a few days later that Cody accidentally stumbled upon the porn that Alan was jerking off to every other night. Cody's eyes went wide when he discovered the sheer number of tickle vids that Alan had stored on his laptop…

ABOUT THE AUTHOR

James T. Medak is a writer and tickle/foot fetish enthusiast of some regard, having previously written *How To Be a Tickle Slave,* a highly-regarded collection of stories, as well as being a frequent contributor to TKL Frat. He currently resides in Chicago.

How To Be a
Tickle Slave

James T. Medak

MEDAK

HOW TO BE A TICKLE SLAVE

A
BONER
BOOK

www.ingramcontent.com/pod-product-compliance
Lightning Source LLC
Chambersburg PA
CBHW051127260626
47170CB00005B/1706